HEZADA!
I MISS YOU

Other works by Erin Pringle:

The Floating Order
The Whole World at Once

HEZADA!
I MISS YOU

Erin Pringle

9.15.20

Hezada! I Miss You

© 2019 Erin Pringle

First Edition

Published by Awst Press
P.O. Box 49163
Austin, TX 78765

awst-press.com
awst@awst-press.org

Printed in the United States of America
Distributed by Small Press Distribution

ISBN: 978-0-9971938-8-6
Library of Congress Control Number: 2019957504

Cover illustration by LK James
Editing by Tatiana Ryckman
Copyediting by Emily Roberts
Book design by LK James

For my family

There is a charge

For the eyeing of my scars, there is a charge
For the hearing of my heart——
It really goes.

And there is a charge, a very large charge
For a word or a touch
Or a bit of blood

Or a piece of my hair or my clothes.

—Sylvia Plath, *Lady Lazarus*

1

It's another hot day, and the petunias have long gone stringy in the baskets that hang from the village's three lampposts. The lampposts stand evenly spaced on the sidewalk in front of the diner. Six lampposts, if you count their reflections in the diner window. More than that if you count their reflections in the empty storefronts across the street.

But if their shadows and reflections don't count as part of their reality, then it's just three.

The lampposts are in the century-ago style closest to the blurry pictures and planning sketches of the village in its youth, when the houses were new, people arrived without leaving, train tracks stitched the land, and advertisements painted the walls of the brick buildings.

The village council bought the lampposts a few years ago when it became hopeful or deluded about tourists: finding them, then luring them into the leaning neighborhoods and brick buildings.

And, once the tourists became residents, the village would be one step closer to having more people under the age of seventy.

Doesn't take a genius to see that it's the children we need to focus on if we want to keep the village here, said a member of the village council at the monthly meeting held in the church basement.

On the folding table in front of the village council was a glossy catalog opened to a page of lampposts. More kinds of lampposts than anyone would imagine. In the audience of folding chairs sat the woman who wrote, edited, and published the village's monthly newsletter.

The refrigerator in the church kitchen stopped groaning.

Please let the minutes reflect that I hereby agree that tourists would invigorate the economy, decrease the village's aging debts.

We've already agreed about that.

But is it in the minutes?

What I want to know is how we charm strangers into moving here when we can't keep people from leaving—people whose families have lived here for generations.

Here we go again.

We're farmers, not real estate agents.

What we need is artists.

Someone laughed into a cough.

I've been reading, said one council member, and as soon as artists move into a place, money follows. In Detroit—

We're not Detroit.

Thank God.

In Chicago…

Everyone groaned.

Here's an idea. Let's ship the crime down from Chicago, and the people will naturally follow.

The men smirked at each other.

You know, Capone sent gin down the Wabash and into Terre Haute.

You'd think Terre Haute would get more tourists for that.

Several nodded.

The newsletter woman took notes.

Who's gonna buy their pictures?

The tourists.

I mean, the artists. Their pictures.

Aren't the tourists moving here?

The refrigerator started mumbling again.

Ideas may be the problem.

Lampposts aren't ideas.

My grandmother would say clean the house first, or you're just decorating dust.

They thought about the train tracks that got pulled up years ago. How the interstate is a good twenty-minute drive one way, or forty minutes another. The village's one school building was torn down a few decades ago, so what kids do live here bus to the nearest town whose heartbeat is a little better.

Tourists will come.

No matter that there's no gas station.

No grocery.

No quick-stop shop, not counting the diner counter of gum and cough drops.

There is a bar.

There is a church, right downtown, and several out in the country.

Listen, don't we all love living here?

I do.

Yes.

And didn't we already agree to invest in our village?

Got to spend money to make money.

Hear, hear.

And didn't we spend most of last year visiting other villages like ours?

Yes, they had, all around the state, and a few rural towns in Indiana and Missouri for good measure. The ones that seemed to thrive resembled ceramic Christmas villages on fuzzy white felt, with their pleasant lighting, stores of organic vegetables, few but friendly taverns all named TAVERN, a shop selling wind chimes, windsocks, full-price hardback children's books, and wire racks of postcards featuring historic pictures of the village. Wine stores, a toy store, maybe. Prices twice higher than anywhere else, but people offer up their credit cards for fair-trade coffee, vegan ice cream, reusable grocery bags printed with sayings about wine, wives, or time. Two, three—even four new restaurants in a village the size of this one.

And a fountain!

Can we just have a water fountain that works year round that ain't clogged with chewing gum?

And the neighborhoods! Everybody's yards the same height and edged with solar-powered light sets.

We already have fines for yards growing higher than six inches.

A local brewery, even.

Next you'll be wanting to allow alcohol on Sundays.

We could renovate the old Ansel house.

But its foundation—

Must be funds for that. A historical society.

Grants.

Loans.

Non-profit status.

Round brass plates stamped with HISTORICAL MARKER.

Ghost Tours.

Wine Tours.

Historical Tours.

The Real Midwest.

Cornfields, soybeans, sadness.

Are you making fun?

Someone could reopen the movie theatre, repair the wiring for the ticket booth lights, dust off the dead spiders, deep-clean the mold, plaster the patches, and darn the rip in the movie screen.

You *are* making fun.

Ideas are the problem.

What we need is something to keep the kids here. Give them something to do. Show them this is a place to stay. Go get your education, sure, but then come back. Raise your families here.

We have a nice park.

We do.

And the circus.

Circus has been coming one hundred summers and the kids have been leaving at least half of those.

I mean, things *like* the circus. There was the skating rink when we were kids.

Kids don't roller skate.

Let the minutes reflect the difficulty of roller skating without a rink.

Maybe you could take this job seriously. Or maybe hope is funny to you.

Revitalization! Beautification! yelled the treasurer and pounded each syllable against the table. As the only woman on the council she often clapped, shouted, or wept—to effect a response or because she felt ideas strongly or because that's what happens in a windowless church basement when you're surrounded by men who think, but never say, you're a pity vote.

No one was sure.

In the end, the council ordered the package of three lampposts.

When the package arrived, no villager volunteered, as hoped, to set up the posts. The box sat in the church basement; after several more meetings, the council agreed to hire someone to sketch blueprints, to draw up permits, to drill into the concrete, to do the wiring, and so forth.

What the council had imagined to be as easy as arranging the annual homecoming festival became a year-long endeavor that ended with a new sidewalk, a new section of street, a revised sewer system, and much more that the newsletter woman omitted to help quell the rising anger about the project, the cost and inconvenience, not to mention how the new sidewalk made the buildings seem, impossibly, wearier.

When the lampposts were erected, the council members gathered around them.

One said, Maybe three isn't enough.

Looks like shit, said another, and spat on the new sidewalk.

Not good for tourists, the council members agreed but didn't say because the same ache blocked all their throats.

Instead, they organized a dedication ceremony and ribbon-cutting to be held on the day the circus arrived. An invitation was sent to the circus boss and his assistant to say a few words. Teenagers were sent down the highway to the town with a stack of posters to hang in the library, gas station, and grocery. They bought ads in the village newsletter, the town newspaper, and the city's university radio station.

They swept the sidewalks.

They stretched a banner across the street.

They threw away the birds that had broken against empty storefronts.

Children carried balloons to the outskirts of the village and tied them to the village's population signs.

Bill's Greenhouse donated the flower baskets for the lampposts. The circus boss gave four big-top tickets to raffle, the florist sold carnations from a card table, and C&M Video gave away one free movie rental. A few villagers grumbled that C&M could have donated an hour of gas money too, for driving all the way to the town and back twice—once for renting, once for return.

The Gibsons hauled in a flatbed with their best tractor, to use as a stage and for the church's sound system.

That day, plenty of people drove the roads that led, one to another, to the village. It was the biggest crowd in years.

People shook hands.

People grabbed each other's elbows and hugged.

People waved, nodded, looked for more faces they knew.

Kids whizzed up and down the length of new sidewalk, and parents shouted to slow down.

A flag was raised.

Last year's homecoming queen sang "The Star-Spangled Banner."

The circus boss lifted his top hat.

His assistant, Frank, waved and did a backflip.

The mayor cut the ribbon.

The lights flickered on inside the lampposts.

Everyone applauded.

Oh, the applause.

Children from Cathy's Dance Studio stood on the flatbed and kick-ball-changed a few numbers. The speakers crackled.

Then came the most beautiful baby pageant, usually reserved for homecoming, but why not today too? You know how people love it. Mothers lifted their babies onto the stage edge and held their babies' knees while laughing to make the babies laugh so the audience laughed.

The pageant judges took notes.

The most beautiful baby was named.

More applause.

Then the circus trucks rolled out to the same field they've set up in every summer since the beginning of time.

The villagers looked at wrappers and plastic bottles left on the new sidewalk.

They looked at the line of people waiting to get into the diner to eat.

They heard the thump-thump of the bass from a passing car.

It's nice to have visitors, but…

There's a reason we never moved to a bigger place.

There's a reason my grandmother never stepped foot beyond the fields.

What are tourists, anyway? Strangers. And what do we know about them, their families? Maybe they're good people, probably they're good people, but it's not like we've got jobs to spare when at least half of us already drive to other towns for work.

If I wanted to live in the city…

If I wanted to lock my doors at night…

If I lived in the city, I'd have some wrong-headed ideas about living in a village, that's for sure.

It's not all lampposts and baby pageants.

It's not a circus every day of the week.

What's wrong with embracing what we have?

I've always felt blessed to have been born here.

There's ups and downs anywhere you live.

According to the village newsletter, the weather for the ribbon-cutting was lovely, and made more enjoyable by this summer's circus setting up by evening. A good time was had by all. As a nice touch, she delayed the obituaries until next newsletter.

Then the circus left.

The crowd left.

The fields were harvested, the kids boarded the school bus to town, the lampposts clicked on each evening and off each morning. The few high school seniors posed under them for their senior pictures, as did a few brides in white gowns and roses in their arms.

And when the village learned the total cost of the three lampposts, all the council members were voted out, and that was that.

2

It's another hot day in the village.

The village's lone traffic light flashes on its wire over the main street. In the heat, the yellow light seems to flash even slower.

Two children turn up the street. It's the twins. Heza and Abe. The girl walks beside the boy, kicking a rock. She's in a swimsuit and cut-offs. The boy's in a shirt and swim trunks. He's on a skateboard and using a crutch to row himself forward. The crutch is taller than he is and has a red mechanic's rag duct-taped to the armrest for a cushion.

The girl kicks the rock. It tumbles ahead over the bumpy street.

The boy lifts the crutch with both hands, sort of leaning it against his shoulder as he tosses it ahead of him. The crutch's tip has lost its rubber cap and clacks against the street, followed by the gritty roll of the skateboard wheels. He tilts his head to keep from thunking his jaw against the crutch again.

The skateboard rolls to a stop. The boy looks up at the sky.

Hey, Heza, he says.

She meets the rock and kicks it again.

Hey, Heza, he says.

She watches the rock skitter right, then left, then land.

You hear it? he says.

She shakes her head.

You sure?

She nods.

He looks over when she doesn't answer, in time to see her chin nod, then go still.

Think it'll be rained out?

She shrugs.

You think that could happen?

Maybe.

Really?

Probably not.

She holds the ends of the bath towel that's rolled up and draped over her neck. It's frayed along the edges and patterned with roses. Abe has one over his shoulders too.

She says, Pool will close if there's lightning, though.

Like last year, he says.

She nods. Might not even open.

Abe thinks about this, then pushes against the crutch. It's harder starting once he's stopped, so he swipes his sneaker against the street for a boost, though it feels like cheating. If he lived in the town instead of the village, he could skateboard on the soft, dark asphalt of the church parking lot near his friend's house. The only church in the village has a small gravel parking lot that's more dust than anything, so mothers are always scolding their kids to pick up your feet when you're walking so you don't ruin your good shoes.

Heza pauses and twists the earring in one ear. Then the other. Both her earlobes hurt. Infected, probably. Her luck. The store lady said to twist the earring posts three times a day to keep the skin from growing over. Because your body thinks it's wounded. Every morning and night she has to press cotton balls against her earlobes, soaked with liquid from a squeeze bottle to prevent infection. The liquid feels cold and good.

You can have short hair, she imagines a witch saying, but *only* if you give me your ear.

Ha ha ha, Heza says and cackles.

What're you doing? Abe says.

Practicing my cackle.

Your what?

Nothing.

Tell me.

No.

Her hair's nearly buzzed, and so much cooler in the heat. It's so hot, the heat's trying to get away from itself but can't, and wavers off the road and up her legs.

You sure you don't hear it? Abe says.

Not yet. Never comes this early in the morning.

Couple weeks ago, Abe was about here when the red truck pulled in, meeting its reflection in the diner window.

Abe listened to Frank and the Summer Boy talking as they climbed out of the truck. Frank was saying, If you're thinking about meeting some girl by the carousel tonight and whisking her down to Florida when we're done, then that's a thought that needs rethinking.

The Summer Boy twisted his lips. I'm not thinking that.

Abe didn't wonder what the Summer Boy's name was. They never have one because they never stay. Then Frank and the Summer Boy were hurrying up the sidewalks, rolling the circus posters up walls.

You're thinking about some girl, Frank said.

There's no girl, said the Summer Boy, and reached into the bed of the truck for the poster boxes.

You're married, Frank said.

I mean, no girl besides mine. I know I'm married. Got kids. That'd be hard to forget.

That's right. Two girls.

Boys, said the Summer Boy.

Don't forget it, Frank said.

Summer Boy rolled his eyes. Abe saw it, but Frank didn't.

In my experience, Frank said, Summer Boys got short memories, or memories that short out. Which kind do you have?

The Summer Boy unfolded the flaps of one box, then another.

Frank unsnapped the container holding the wheat paste.

Bring your kids to Florida instead of some carousel girl. Your kids ever been to the beach?

The Summer Boy shook his head.

Lots of seashells. So many seashells you never know which ones washed up this morning and another morning, unless, as I figure it, you take them home every day, and how can you do that? I mean, even if you could, would the knowing be worth it?

Are you asking me? said the Summer Boy.

Frank didn't answer.

Abe's only seen seashells on his grandmother's necklaces or in the canning jars on her dresser.

You collect anything? said Frank as he followed the Summer Boy to the brick wall of the building that was the clothing store, then laundromat, then grocery, and now empty.

The Summer Boy held up the poster. Frank rolled the paste up the back of it. The Summer Boy flipped it, and Frank rolled over it once more.

It's good to collect something, Abe heard Frank say. Buttons, seashells, blue bottles to keep the bad spirits away.

Not girls, though, the Summer Boy said.

Frank laughed. That's right. Live long enough and you'll see girls wash up like seashells.

The rest of the village kids had started trickling in to watch the posters go up and see what they looked like this year.

Frank and the Summer Boy moved down the sidewalk, dipping posters and rolling them up.

The Summer Boy nodded.

Didn't take long to announce what everybody knew anyway, since the circus has been visiting for more than a century, and as soon as the men broke down the cardboard boxes, tossed them into the truck, and drove away, Abe and the other kids were rushing the buildings, peeling down the posters, and hurrying home, hoping to reach their bedrooms before the paste dried.

And for the last two weeks, Abe's awoken to the poster, then gone to the kitchen calendar to cross off another day until the circus arrives.

And now.

Now.

This is the day. Here we are. Only thing left is to hear the circus music coming up the way, or maybe see the circus campers and trucks first, from here, or better, from the top of the high-dive.

Don't rain, Abe whispers to the sky. Don't you do it.

3

A raindrop lands on the camper windshield and beads, rolling down the country road that passes in the side mirror.

Frank pretends not to notice.

Another raindrop.

Another.

It'd be good for the rain to hold off, though the damp air rushing through the camper windows means rain's coming no matter. Probably rain was in the forecast, but Frank rarely turns on the small TV in his camper. Were others talking about the weather while tearing down camp? He can't recall. When the circus is packing or unpacking, he's in automatic mode and hardly aware of what's around him.

Another raindrop hits the windshield and beads, its shadow rolling across the reflection of Frank's cheek.

Another.

He glances at the shadows of the raindrops moving against the dashboard. Not enough to trigger the wipers.

He rests his hand on the armrest and checks the side mirror. The red truck and the rest of the caravan are still following him, like the fields and the road. In dreams, he looks into the same side mirror, and nobody's following except the road, empty and travelling away from him.

Those are good dreams.

He lifts his hand. The boy in the red truck waves. The boy hasn't tripped his wipers either. Few months ago, the wipers would be slinging back and forth. Kid's learning.

Your job is to be my shadow, Frank said.

A taller one, maybe, the boy said.

A younger Frank would have grimaced. This far into life he doesn't, though he does feel the ghost of the grimace pulling at his face. He used to blame himself for jokes like that.

The Summer Boy started to apologize, and Frank didn't stop him, which seemed to surprise the Summer Boy.

Frank's learned that it's fine for other people to feel uncomfortable. He learned that on his own, since his mother couldn't teach it, seeing as how she believed it was her duty to make everyone feel comfortable, at ease.

Anyway, that was the last the Summer Boy said of Frank's height.

To him, anyway.

Every year, the circus boss warns the Summer Boys before hiring them to keep their traps shut, but it happens anyway. It's only two things I'm asking you to do, the circus boss will say. Keep your traps shut about Frank's height, number one. And number, two, stay away from the town girls. Can you do that?

Sure, they say.

I mean it, he says.

Absolutely.

Every summer I sigh and say this, and every Summer Boy sits there and says, I hear you, sir.

I mean it, sir. I hear you.

And probably the Summer Boys do mean it. They're successful for the first, maybe the second setup, show, and teardown. Then they start feeling comfortable, or start seeing how hard it is to keep people on, which means their job's secure. And then a joke slips. A comment. A comment flipped into a joke so that it can be shrugged off, dismissed, made to seem like Frank's just an overly sensitive guy.

Frank never tells the boss, though.

Fire the sons of bitches, the circus boss would say.

Even Frank's former schoolteachers would say he needed thicker skin. Because you *are* shorter, Frankie.

Don't call me Frankie, he'd think.

Can't expect them not to notice, can you, Frankie?

Frank.

Different is different, and sorry to say, you are. But everyone has a cross, and maybe it's just learning how to bear it.

And he believed it because he loved his teachers, and because everyone around him seemed to agree with them.

Years later, after the internet began and everything came with a comment board, he read all the nasty things people would say. He felt vindicated. People did think exactly as he'd imagined.

So, turns out, Frank was just everybody's internet article all those years. Or something like it. He's not sure. It's tempting to call the whole damn internet a circus, but it's only the same if you've never lived in one.

What's the difference?

Well, there's no sequins.

He chuckles.

Back when he was a kid, no one hung motivational posters saying MARCH TO YOUR OWN DRUMMER. First time he saw advice like that, he thought they were jokes like he was used to. When he realized they weren't, he wept.

Fuuuuck.

But here we are, folks, last set for the summer, and last set ever for him. Frank's retiring in three days, once the last tent is packed up.

Wherever he goes, people will notice. That's an old thought, and now it's back. But you stay long enough somewhere, they get used to it. If they don't, well, he could move on, or he could bloody their noses—as a kid, he once busted another boy's eardrum on the playground. That's what it takes sometimes, maybe no matter your age.

How's that for a motivational poster?

His eyebrows rise like a laugh, which is how he usually laughs since sound draws attention, and by this time in life, he's wired to avoid it.

Here's more raindrops, sounding on the camper roof like the pebbles he used to toss into the creek from the bridge near his childhood home.

Another country road comes out of the fields and meets this road. Then it's in his rear-view mirror. Then gone. Same thing happens in the red truck's rear-view. And the car behind it. And the truck behind the car, and on down to the last trailer in the caravan—the one lugging the wooden carousel that's whirled above fields in the rural Midwest since eighteen-hundred-something. Same carousel where Frank hid the first time he tried running away from home.

This rain isn't going to stop.

He stretches out his fingers, then drums them gently against the steering wheel.

Shouldn't he be done caring about this by now? You're an old man, Frank. This is your last circus, your last show.

Thinking about it isn't caring, is it?

Maybe his pending retirement is what's bringing it all back. Every year like a piece of tissue paper, one laid one on top of another, like those tissue flowers Hezada used to make, and now after enough pieces, even tissue paper goes opaque. And now he's pulling them apart again, one by one.

Love me, love me not.

Love's got nothing to do with it.

But wouldn't that be something?—to bloody the mouth of the last Summer Boy he works with—after decades of turning his cheek until he's dizzy, decades of shows, of Summer Boys patting his head or winking over it at town girls, summer after summer of fathers and grandfathers singing drunkenly up sleeping streets and into the circus field after midnight, whether the circus is camping there or not. Frankie, where are you? Frankie, tell me how the circus's been. Singing the song that will be sung about him long after he dies.

Decades of laughs, quips, raised eyebrows, open stares, glares, not-looking-but-looking looks. But this summer, on the very last day of the circus, he'll just knock the Summer Boy clean out, teeth clinking to the dirt like cartoon piano keys.

He raises his eyebrows.

Of course, he won't be hitting one Summer Boy but fifty years of Summer Boys and gawkers and taffy winders and glass-eyed animals strung from striped awnings—and it's all of them falling to the ground at once, eyes snapping open in the skull of one boy hitting the ground.

Then Frank will crouch down beside the body, hold out a paper cup to spit the blood into.

No, he won't do that. Doesn't even want to.

Maybe in his younger days.

But he didn't punch anybody in his younger circus days either. Plenty of audience members happy to do the fighting, and plenty of performers happy to oblige.

In those good old days that you hear about. Those days smelled like blood and sawdust too. Animal shit and sweat.

Of course, maybe he didn't throw a punch because the circus, the audiences, everyone did pretty thorough work of making him believe that they saw him for who he was. And they didn't see a fighter. They didn't line up at his tent because they'd see him the same as they'd see the world's strongest man.

Whoever he was then.

He's just not that now.

Frank and his therapist have talked about that. People change. You've got to allow that in yourself too. Maybe now is the first time he's fully felt an ability to push back, a need to push back, a revulsion and wish that have just now bloomed.

He imagines himself punching the Summer Boy in the jaw.

Summer Boy would probably knock him out, quick as reflex.

Then it'd be Frank on the ground, looking up.

But would the moment be worth it?

The circus boss would come to see about the commotion and appear above Frank.

So, he'd say.

So, Frank would say.

Helluva ride.

Yes.

Then the boss would extend his hand, crucifix tattoo showing for a second, and help Frank up. And if ritual is anything to rely on, they'd find the nearest tavern and drink to their last circus together.

You sure you're not coming back next season? the boss would say again.

That's right, Frank would say. Again.

Well, it's been a heck of a ride, the two of us.

And it has. It has. Spent more of their lives together than most married couples, which they note when another set of friends or celebrities announces they're breaking up.

Though sometimes Frank wonders whether the circus boss imagines him more like a son, but the sort you hear about—who grows up working the family farm, bar, business, but despite promising to pass it down to him, the father never does, and the business and father die together.

That love story.

But didn't the circus boss tell him he needn't work the tents like that anymore?

Well, sort of.

Not really.

No.

The circus boss did give Frank pep talks about acting. What actor doesn't wonder who he himself is? Name one, Frank. Name two. Even the best performers worry their characters are more praiseworthy, more interesting, more everything than who they themselves are offstage, in jeans, at a coffee shop, a laundromat, in bed, saying nothing or saying much more, but with fewer listeners and no applause.

Frank would nod and try to think like that. He tried to make it simply a philosophical problem in order to ignore the growing chasm between who he was in the tent and who he was outside of it.

He did a good job ignoring it.

4

And then the nausea started. The circus gates would open, and grit of sickness and ache would crawl around Frank's chest, chew on his heart, yawn through his bones.

The crowds surged in.

Up and down the midway, the hawkers, talkers, handlers began their songs—from one tent to another, one stage to the next—

COME SEE THE UGLIEST—

THE STRANGEST—

COME SEE, COME SEE

THE MOST—THE SMALLEST—THE INCREDIBLE—

FOLKS, LET ME TELL YOU

A SECRET

A MARVEL

LET ME CHANGE THE WORLD AS YOU KNOW IT.

And Frank would walk from his camper to the tent.

HERE IS THE ACT—

Frank crouched behind the tent, elbows on knees, dry-heaving.

Until the morning came when he woke up and felt as though his mass had doubled, tripled, as though the Sandman had come in the night, stuck a funnel in Frank's mouth, and filled him with bags of sand.

He did not feel like even trying to get out of bed.

Surely, his new mass would deflate the camper tires. The circus would have to leave without him. His camper would sink, one rainfall at a time.

How warm and dark the field would be if he were inside it.

How safe.

How preferable to walking into that tent again, in a ruff to recite *Hamlet*

…in a flying suit for the cannon.

…in boxing gloves to fight a rooster, a pit bull, the tallest man who lifts him in one hand.

…in a pram pushed by a clown in a dress. The clown waves; the audience waves back. Clearly, the clown's a man with a pillow for breasts.

The clown squirts the flower on his dress into the pram, like he's feeding the baby in there.

The audience giggles.

The clown takes out a compact, a makeup brush. The clown looks into the tiny mirror.

Then, bam! Frank pops from the pram, wearing only a bonnet and diaper, and grabs the clown's pillow breasts with both hands.

The clown shouts and jumps. Frank jumps out of the pram and runs. The clown gives chase. The clown's dress is unzipped in the back, showing polka-dot pantaloons.

Oh, how the crowd loved it!

How the crowd leaned in!

How the crowd shouted for the clown to catch Frank, for Frank to escape the clown.

How funny for men to be women.

How demoralizing!

How ridiculous!

How awful it's funny!

The day Frank woke up filled with sand, he did not leave the camper.

Instead, he pulled the blanket tighter around his shoulders. He stared out the camper's screen window. He slept. He stared.

And the next day like that.

And the next.

Until no one had seen Frank for three nights in a row. Hezada came by to check on him. She knocked. He didn't answer. She came around to the camper's screen window where his bed was.

Frank, she said.

Hezada, he said.

Circus is leaving.

Okay.

I see you, she said.

He nodded.

I can hitch your camper to mine, if you want. You don't need to help.

I'll help.

No, she said. You rest.

So he did, though he didn't think rest was what he was doing.

At the next stop, he returned to the tent.

The summer passed. The bookkeeper quit or was fired, and Frank learned how to do the job.

Another summer passed. The boss had to lay off the two secretaries who ran marketing and communications.

Frank learned those jobs too.

Then the band.

Oh, the band.

But he took over the sound systems.

And then he stopped performing.

One evening while the boss and he sat under the camper awning drinking iced tea, the boss said, Isn't it about time for your act? To get ready?

I don't do that now, Frank said.

The boss nodded and didn't say more. And they've never talked about the days Frank worked inside tents. The boss hasn't apologized, or known how to apologize, or why an apology might be in order. Boss has lived the circus as long as Hezada. His father ran it before him. Even if he and Frank spoke of it, boss would say there was more abuse back then. There's less now. What do you want? This isn't no Betty Ford clinic. We'd make more money if it were, and most everyone would qualify. Are we supposed to apologize to the audiences for seeing what they saw, and not seeing what they didn't?

Frank doesn't speak of those times to anyone. Even when he found himself in a dental chair, and the dentist told him he was missing most of the enamel on his teeth. Do you know why that may be?

Your guess is as good as mine, Frank said.

You ever suffered from acid reflux? Heartburn?

Something like that, Frank said and stared into the very bright light.

5

Heza picks up the rock and pockets it.

Abe's trying to jump the skateboard over the curb so he can roll along the new section of sidewalk.

Heza cranes to see the red boots in the thrift store window. She's tried on the boots every day since she and their mother lifted them from a box of donations, which is the only good part about helping their mother at the thrift store.

Look! Heza had exclaimed.

There two of them? her mother said, digging around for the other.

There were, and Heza took them, turning them over, running her thumb over the stitching, pressing them against her heart.

They're falling apart, her mother said.

I love them, Heza said.

Go ahead and put them on the shoe rack.

Instead, Heza sat down and kicked off her sneakers. Her socks didn't match, which her mother noticed.

Lord, Heza, her mother said.

What? Heza said, though she knew exactly what her mother was Lord-ing.

You know what.

Heza pulled at the loops until her heel thudded into the boot, then the next. They felt tight around the toes, but if she said that, her mother would definitely say no.

They fit!

Her mother rolled her eyes.

They do.

Then come over here and let me feel the toes.

They fit. Why don't you trust me?

Heza.

Mom.

Go put them on the shoe rack when you're done pretending they fit.

Please let me have them.

They're falling apart, Heza. Must be older than me.

Then why you selling them if they're so awful? Heza turned on one toe, then the other. She started to slip but righted herself.

Because, her mother said, whoever donated them expects them sold. Somebody could buy inserts for them, maybe. Or take them down to the shoe repairman, have new soles put on.

So could we, Heza said.

New soles won't make them fit you. Too expensive, anyway, even if they did.

If nobody buys them in a month, can I have them?

Her mother didn't answer.

Heza loves how they clickety-clack against the concrete floor of the thrift store, loves twisting on her toe, then dropping into a crouch and holding out her hands like a gun, aiming them at the girl in red boots aiming back from the rectangular mirror drilled into the wall.

It's a draw.

Again.

Probably the boots are from the circus. Maybe a leatherwork-er joined for a season and sold them to all the kiddos on the route.

Salesmen do that: join for a season, then leave. There's other things in the thrift store from past circuses. Kazoos pasted with clown-face stickers. Tin drums. Headdresses. Clown shoes with split soles. Black and white 8x10s signed by performers, conjoined twins, women with beards, elephants on their rear legs, men with mustaches balancing women shaped like applause on their hands, Hezada the Great in her peacock costume, or Hezada's mother—also Hezada—in the same peacock costume, leaping to catch the trapeze bar with one hand.

Abe likes to collect the circus junk. When their mother lost her job at the bank because the bank left the village, she started working at the thrift store. Abe couldn't have been more pleased. Just think, he will marvel from time to time, what my collection would be like if you always worked here.

Mmm, their mother will say.

Awesome is what it would be.

Probably, their mom will say, if she answers.

The bank clock still hangs off the corner of the old bank building, and it worked until a few years ago—first falling an hour behind because of daylight savings, then two hours, then stopping completely. Nobody knows how long it was broken before the villagers realized nobody could fix it.

6

The felt on the camper's ceiling ripples above Frank's head. But even with the wind and the threat of rain, it's damn hot. Camper's AC broke a couple years back, but since only July and August are bad, fixing seems a waste. Rest of the year, the weather's heating up or cooling down, or he's in Florida where the circus hibernates all winter. And when he does remember the AC's broken, it's already damn hot, he's in a foul mood, and who would fix it? Any mechanic around here would have to order the parts—if the parts are made anymore, and if they are, they won't arrive until Frank's five, six towns away. Which, added to the stares he'll get in any mechanic shop, just isn't worth it.

Of course they notice, Frankie. They can't help that.

But when it's hot and his temper's jagged, it's harder to accommodate people who take one look and ask, Is the circus in town?

Well, fuck you, he says. He hits the wipers.

The boy in the truck hits his too.

Fuck. You. Fuck. You. That's the rhythm of the wipers. Fuck. You.

Sure, the circus is why he's here, but it's the assumption. The way the stares zip him into a life that's not his. He was born around here, just like them, which he could say but doesn't. If he'd stayed around here, though, and never joined the circus, people from here would still see him and assume the circus must be close. Because every summer for a hundred and more years the circus has come and brought men and women like him with it.

Which is why he left home when he did, though he was young— eight or nine years old. Maybe he should have waited. It wears him out to think too hard about it. He has reached an age that feels far from the sea of his own time. He didn't notice it happening until he said Back in My Day, and a Summer Boy rolled his eyes.

But it's true. Like his mother would say, In my day, people didn't French kiss or curse in movies, and everything else was a secret.

Maybe people were just better at keeping secrets.

Maybe the circus tents were simply an echo of that.

There's one last stretch of road before the final curve that winds like a woman's leg folded beneath her, and into the village where the speed limit drops and trees gather.

It isn't a long drive to the village from the last town. But twenty minutes between rural towns is different time to villagers than a twenty-minute drive is for city folk. Most people around here don't like a drive that long. Seems like a big trip, one to steal most of your morning. One you've got to plan for.

He thinks of his little apartment near the ocean. Its green kitchen counters. The windsock he bought up here and hung from the porch down there. The sound of the ocean beating at the windows, promising to crumble the building one day, just through steadiness. The steady force of me, says the ocean, will crumble you.

But, Frank, that place isn't yours anymore.

That's right.

Now it's empty of his stuff. Probably full of new things. In fact, he knows it is because the landlord confused moving days, and Frank woke to a family of five standing in his bedroom doorway, mouths open, and holding the keys to his apartment.

Our apartment, they said.

My apartment, Frank said.

Shit, said the landlord.

His apartment, all those years he lived there, is now packed into this camper or being sorted at the thrift store where he took the rest. First summer in years he hasn't had a home to think of. Maybe that's why he's thinking of his childhood home more. He doesn't like this feeling of floating untied.

Untied? That doesn't seem right.

Untethered. Seems like untethered was an answer to one of the circus boss's crosswords a few years ago. He can't remember the clue.

You can go back, he thinks. Get a better place, better view. Or the same shit place with a worse view. Become friends with the family in your apartment, celebrate birthdays with them, look after their kids, sleep with the wife, play pool with the husband.

Fuck. You. Fuck. You.

As though life works like that.

Maybe for some.

Not for Frankie, though. He needs a thick skin and not to be surprised by people surprised at him.

The windshield wipers smear the dirt and dust from the last fairground. Hopefully, it's not a staying rain. Hopefully, gone by noon and without delaying setup, which once took a full day but not anymore. Now, they'll be unpacked and raised by late afternoon—with time for daylight and a dip in the public pool, unless lightning closes the pool early, all the kiddies hurrying home in towels and wet hair, terrified and curious about being struck by lightning.

Of course, it'd be better if setup still took the whole day. Because that'd mean the circus was still big. More tents. More acts. More money. More noise, commotion, movement, cries of COME SEE THE TALLEST MAN, THE HUMAN CANNONBALL, THE MOST DEATH-DEFYING ACT OF THIS CENTURY. The easier to disappear into the laughter, the lights, the crowds, the ready-made costumes, and the fears and absurdities the circus welcomes everyone into. The circus works, as long as everyone in the rings and bleachers believes they're sharing the same good time.

The bigger the circus, the easier it is for the clowns to fall and to fall for the clowns.

But a circus like that means he's back walking the plank between his camper and the tent, blindfolded so he doesn't know which end falls over the ocean.

Thing is, by this point in his life, it can't matter anymore. It can't.

He's retiring, isn't he? Yes. And so in a matter of days, he will enter a whole new phase of life, a new moon to live by. He'll meet brilliant women, learn new songs, paint every sunset over the last one.

You don't have to retire, you know, the circus boss said.

Because you can't live without me, Frank said.

Funny. But we're friends, aren't we? Won't you miss this? The circus, Frank. The circus.

Tell you what, I'll stay *if* this circus starts travelling the country.

The boss sighed.

I mean it.

It's the only way he'd feel comfortable traveling the country. Hell, he'd even volunteer. See the sights in a way he's used to. The old nausea returns when he imagines vacationing with one of those travel-company tours. On a tour bus. Taking pictures. Buying souvenirs. Eating lunch at hotels with retired lawyers, day-job people, health-insurance people, people who own artificial Christmas trees. Imagine that.

What would he even say to people like that?

Maybe people like that aren't all bad.

Maybe they don't all buy tickets to the circus.

Maybe if they go to the circus, they don't all prowl the tents at the end of the midway.

Maybe they don't all leer or whistle or pretend to puke.

Anyhow, isn't that how they were told to behave? Weren't they taught what a monstrosity was, then encouraged to come see it? What secrets of the universe did anyone expect a circus tent to hold? But isn't it beautiful that people wanted to know them?

What futures did the palm reader map on their hands? It's beautiful, isn't it, that for a dollar and a glass-blown second, a farm boy can see for the first time a life for himself unlike all the lives around him?

And what of the revivalists rolling along on their own roadside tours, unfurling their own tents of desire and sin, miracles and devils?

Frank thinks it's probably a double bind.

Even if a circus still did travel the entire country, it would look like this one. Fewer everything. One elephant. One or two tightrope walkers. A handful of acrobats. A quartet of clowns. One tattooed woman. One disfigured performer, once known as Hezada the Great, who flew on the trapeze and applause and after the show signed glossy 8x10s of herself just as her mother and her mother's mother had under the same name.

Hezada.

But then the cancer found her like it does most everybody these days, and the surgeons removed her breasts and more—tissue, muscles, and whatever else was in her upper arms that could have gotten more cancer.

The doctors called it a radical mastectomy.

An operation performed more regularly, evidently, a hundred years ago.

An operation that would take her ability to catch her body weight on a trapeze bar.

A rare operation for a rare lady, Frank said to her.

You trying to cheer me up? she said.

Maybe.

7

When Hezada was recovering from the operation, she and Frank would walk down to the beach together. Once she wasn't afraid of the sand getting into everything, places she couldn't see but imagined as wounds in the war movies she'd seen in her life.

I feel like I know you better now, she said to him.

He squinted. Because you feel like you don't fit?

Maybe.

I don't think I've ever felt like you, he said.

Did you ever want children? she said.

It would have been alright.

You would have been a good dad.

You're not the first woman to say so.

She laughed.

He watched her turn a seashell over with her toe. The sand tucked inside it.

He said, I don't think I've ever asked if you wanted children.

Typically, people don't ask gay people if they want children.

I never thought to, I guess.

And that's probably why they don't ask.

He thought about this.

Anyway, I don't know, said Hezada. Yes and no. I'd have these nagging desires.

And that stopped when y—

When I realized I was gay?

Yeah.

Well, everything felt different. I don't know, Frank. How could I have a child when it took me so long to know who I was? I mean, Jesus, Frank. Gay people weren't even sideshows.

What made you bring up kids, anyway? he said.

She pressed the shell into the sand and covered it. I was wondering whether women who nursed have a harder time with this kind of operation. Or women who have been assaulted, you know? Just slice the trauma right off. She wove her hands like knives.

Right off, he said.

Yep.

So how do you feel about it?

She glanced at him, then back at the ocean. She touched her lips, then shook her head.

The waves came in. Then rushed out.

It's okay to have a hard time with it, he said.

She nodded those little nods of hers that meant she was upset.

It's only the circus, he said.

She laughed, and tears came down her cheeks.

Right, she said. That's all. Just the circus.

Just the circus.

It's a circus out there, she said.

What a circus, he said.

Son of a circus, she said.

I'll circus you up.

She leaned down. Will you? she said.

He reached up and pushed her tears away with his hands.

We've been through a lot, she said.

Yes, he said.

I mean me and my breasts.

Yes, he said.

It's a joke, she said.

I understand that kind of joke, he said.

She looked out at the ocean. The waves came and came.

I can't help but think of my own death when I'm at the ocean, Frank said.

Did you know that the word circus once meant death?

You're kidding, he said.

Yeah.

They laughed.

I wish you wouldn't come back, Frank told her. Once you're better.

Sure, I'll just call bingo down at the VFW. Maybe I'll take up pottery.

Frank shrugged. Nothing wrong with pottery.

Maybe a cruise.

Cruises are relaxing, I hear.

Cruises only happen in health-insurance land. That glorious land of 401(k)s. Pensions. Stock options. You've heard of it?

Up ahead, a child was building a sandcastle.

Listen, she said, I can't be ashamed to change tents. Shame can't have anything to do with it. It's a job, and I've got bills. Big bills. The biggest bills in all the world, Frank.

He didn't laugh.

Or whatever. Anyway, the new act will probably be surprisingly similar. Tents and lights. Music. A stage.

No, he said.

She looked at his face and saw the summers he was remembering. She said, You'll tell them how to think of me. We'll figure how to sell it.

He shook his head.

She slowly, and with pain, stretched out her arms, as though raising a banner. Come see the most beautiful woman! she said.

Frank tried to think of how to put words on standing alone in that tent. When he stopped performing, friends talked loudly so he'd hear them say Frank thinks he's so much better now. If he's so much better, why's he still hanging around?

And if it doesn't work, Hezada said, then it doesn't work. Then maybe I'll have flowers tattooed over them, tiger lilies and roses, clouds and clotheslines. Camouflage myself as a garden. Become an objet d'art.

An objet d'art?

She smiled. She kicked some sand on his feet. Why not? You know, I've always liked that white and blue design on china dishes. Perhaps I'll have Old Joe tattoo me into that.

You want to look like a plate? Frank said.

Yes, Frank. I'll be a plate, and you can dress up as a spoon.

Who will be the cow?

Circus boss. Shoot him over a cardboard moon.

Hell, why not the real moon?

That'll bring the crowds back.

For sure, she said.

Listen, she said, worst case, I'm selling tickets in a booth or leading the kiddies around on pony rides.

That rate, you'll never retire.

Frankie, you're the only one dreaming of retiring from the circus. Circus has never worked that way, even if the circus boss stuck that in your head to make you work longer.

It's not like that.

In some ways, she went on, there's something beautiful about it, that you can wish your life into something like that.

You're being kind of an asshole.

I'm just telling you what I think.

Same.

Listen, before you showed up on the scene, a lot more went on than a woman without tits shaking it in a tent, I'll tell you that.

I know. I just.

You're looking out for me, and I appreciate that. But I am not Hezada the Great. I have never been Hezada the Great.

I understand that.

Then who do I need to explain it to? What is wrong with Hezada the Great having cancer and losing her breasts like I have?

I'm not the one to be angry at.

8

The nurse unicycles into the tent wearing a white suit and cap. She honks her red, round nose. She waves at the kids in the audience.

Hezada stands on a tower of plywood crates. How did she get up there without a ladder? On the back of a large bird? Perhaps someone stacked the crates beneath her?

Hezada looks out at the audience from beneath a veil that drapes her head to toe. Beneath the veil, her chest is bound with bandages.

Watch closely.

Blood blooms through the fabric. Bright reds. Dried maroons. Carnations, roses, scabs, cardinals. Pus too. The color of pine.

How typically she bleeds!

The nurse parks her unicycle and climbs the stage.

Frank enters through the curtains. They glitter in the light. He clears his throat. He looks past the stage, into the tent lights. He says, We are gathered here today.

The nurse slips from her climb and falls to the ground. She laughs. She shrugs. She honks her nose. She climbs again.

The crates shift.

The audience gasps.

When the nurse reaches Hezada, she stands beside her. The nurse lifts the veil and begins to loosen the bandages.

Your fingers are cold, Hezada says.

I'm sorry, the nurse says.

Show us! a man yells from the audience.

Yeah! Move it!

The nurse says, You are healing nicely.

Thank you.

The nurse lowers the veil.

But nurse…

The nurse turns back.

Help me.

9

When Frank ran away the first time, Hezada found him after her show, hiding in the carousel shadows, crouched by the hooves of a wooden horse. Hezada must have been sixteen or seventeen at the time.

In the distance, Frank's mother was trying to shout his name without making the crowd feel uncomfortable.

Are you *that* Frankie? said Hezada the Great. That your mom?

He looked up at her.

She stooped down beside him. She was still wearing her green sequined costume, peacock plumes sewn into the back. She smelled like the circus.

Frankie? she said.

Frank, he said.

Wanna know a secret, Frank? she said.

He nodded.

She smiled. Even in the shadows, he could see the makeup on her face. Small gems pasted to her forehead.

You see these feathers? she said and turned so that the peacock feathers shifted with the movement. Did you know that real peacocks, like the sort these feathers come from, are male?

He watched her.

But I'm female, she said. That's funny, right? She smiled.

He smiled.

You know what's even funnier?

He didn't.

This was my mother's costume. So am I dressed up like my mother or a peacock?

I don't know.

Me neither, she said. I wonder what it would be like to have a peacock for a mother.

He watched her, not knowing what to think.

He couldn't hear his mother calling his name anymore. He listened. Then his mother's voice started up again, calling for him, but quieter, more unsure.

Can I tell you something else? said Hezada.

He nodded, more readily now.

If you're running away, this is not how you want to do it.

I'm not, he said.

Okay, kitten, but if you are, this is not how to. Trust me. Go home. Come back when you know what you're doing. Bet you don't even have a suitcase. Do you?

He shook his head.

Well, then. She held out her hand. He gave her his. They both stood, and she walked him away from the carousel and through the crowd until she could wave down his mother. The look on his mother's face.

He's never forgotten it.

Long after he was reunited with his mother, he could feel the heat of Hezada's hand in his. Long after he and his mother got home and sat in silence on the couch. Long after he went to bed, and the stars blinked out. He fell asleep with his hands clasped.

When he ran away the next summer, he brought a suitcase.

10

Hezada walks from her camper to the tent. She wears her old sequined costume, her tights, those feathers. The tent is near the end of the midway. She waits in the grass behind the curtain.

At the tent's entrance, Frank calls people to see Hezada the Great! Hezada!

The men and the women file in. More women than you'd think.

When it's time, Frank moves to stand inside the tent.

He starts the recording of "Entrance of the Gladiators." He aims a spotlight on the curtain. The people quiet down.

Hezada comes out.

Frank imagines swallowing the circus like the fire-eater opening his mouth to flame.

11

COME SEE THE SADDEST WOMAN IN THE VILLAGE.

HURRY!

12

Kae looks up as her children walk through the door of the thrift store.

Is it here yet? she says.

Almost, Abe says.

Heza licks her finger and holds it in the air. Wind's eastways, she says.

Hey, says Abe, because he said the exact same thing a moment ago, but when he said it, he consulted his broken pocket watch. And it was funnier.

Their mother laughs.

That's my joke, Abe says.

But Heza's already crouched on the floor and pulling on a red boot.

Abe climbs onto the chair behind the glass counter where his mother usually sits. He rests his forehead on it and looks down through the glass shelves. There's a tin drum and a green glass necklace adorning a headless velvet throat. He rocks his forehead so that the necklace glitters in the fluorescent lights above him.

He thinks of the glittery circus ladies who ride the backs of the horses. Maybe this one time Mom will buy front-row tickets—so close he'll reach out and touch the bellies of the horses as they pass, like he used to touch the grocery shelves as their mother pushed him in the cart.

If they have front-row seats, the audience can't stop him from scrambling into the ring and jumping onto one of the horses. A circus lady will hold him around the waist to keep him from falling and breaking his neck.

The crowd will gasp. They'll crane their necks to see better. They'll cover their eyes.

Is this part of the act?

Look at that! Would you look at that!

Is that Abe?

Our Abe?

Can't be.

No, that's Heza.

Well, they *are* twins.

Not with that hair.

Didn't you know she had it buzzed off?

Wait, that is Abe!

Our Abe!

Now everyone's on their feet.

Abe waves.

Abe! Abe!

He stands on the saddle, his body light as a kite rustling here and there in the breeze.

The audience clasps their hearts. The horses gallop, dust poofs, the tent lights blur like the carousel's when it's really going.

That boy, did you see that?

What?

Abe, that charming boy, can you believe it, just changed into a tuxedo right there on the back of the horse.

That's no horse. That's a giraffe.

No, a lion.

Two lions. Abe is riding on the backs of two lions! Can you believe it?

A giraffe and a lion.

AMAZING! What balance! What grace! What strength!

Abe holds out his top hat, flipping it into the air—

AND THEN HE CATCHES IT!

ON HIS HEAD!

They clap and cheer and call his name over and over.

What are you smiling about? Heza says. He can see through the glass counter to the red boots she's wearing. The boots are too small, but he doesn't say it.

13

Up ahead is the blue house Frank passes every summer, windows around the front like a greenhouse. He always tries to see whether there's plants in there, but the road or lighting changes so he can't. The tree in the front yard used to hold a tire swing.

Blue house is the last house before the village. Roadside, anyway. Most houses out here sit deeper in the fields, or beyond the windbreaks, off gravel roads and not this main road.

He glances in the side mirror. The Summer Boy sees him and nods. Frank nods back, then slows to make sure the Summer Boy slows down too. Young boys don't like to slow down. That's just the way. Even this one, even if he does have a wife and kids.

Summer Boys drive fast because they know so little. Or something like that. Or they think their current lives are pretend and that their real lives are waiting up ahead, and if they go a little faster, they'll reach their real lives faster. He felt that way once. Seems like most of the Summer Boys think like that. Maybe girls do too, but they've never had a Summer Girl. Summer Girls are the town girls who are supposed to stay away from the Summer Boys, but don't.

He slows the camper more. There's some power in it. Take power where you can, long as you aren't hurting anybody.

Probably the Summer Boys don't hold it against him for driving slow. Probably think his camper's just so damn old the engine can't handle it.

Which is true, just not fully true.

This Summer Boy has pictures of his wife and kids clipped to a hair ribbon tied to his rear-view mirror.

You're kidding me, Frank said when he saw it.

My wife made it, the boy said.

Of course she did, Frank said.

Little red hearts were drawn down the ribbon.

The Summer Boy said, She used to be a Brownie or Camp Fire Girl. One of those.

Frank nodded.

She's afraid I'll forget her, said the Summer Boy. I love her. With all my heart.

Okay, Frank said.

You don't believe me.

Frank squinted and pressed his tongue against the roof of his mouth. I like to believe, Frank said. I'd *love* to believe. That's not the issue. Frank shrugged. But soon as somebody tells me I need to believe, I get a little worried. My spine starts to tingle. You ever have that feeling? Like a cat raising up inside you ever so slowly.

The Summer Boy nodded slowly.

Frank nodded too, and waited for the boy to understand. He'd had about the same conversation with most every Summer Boy, even the ones not married to Girl Scouts. But he thought he shouldn't tell the boy that. May not be good for a kid to hear that his mistakes are the same as everybody's. Might be good to believe every suffering has a clear cause and that mistakes aren't waiting for your birth like lights for moths.

Anyhow, that's been about the longest exchange between him and this year's Summer Boy, thankfully. Some Summer Boys like to talk a lot, and he can feel it, even when they're quiet, like a faucet turned to the edge of on.

Maybe after this last set of shows, this boy will return home instead of trying to follow the circus to Florida. Some Summer Boys last a whole winter, if the ocean's novelty is enough, and it doesn't bother them to work as line cooks down there same as they would up here, but even then they usually don't last and wind up returning to the Midwest long before spring.

Sometimes, Frank'll see the Summer Boys again, back in their hometowns, strolling the midway beneath the strings of lights. Girls on their arms, military boots on their feet.

It's still damn brave to leave the place you're from, even if you leave it because you hate it—or hate it so you can leave it. And it's even harder to stay left, especially when you can't go back in any real way.

Maybe Frank'll visit his mother a little longer this time, maybe even longer than that winter of her cancer when he stayed a month.

I'm gonna stay sick so you'll stay longer, she'd said to him.

Jesus, Mother.

It's true.

Don't talk like that.

You're keeping me alive.

Chemo's keeping you alive.

Chemo's killing me like it did Joe Wilson. You remember Joe Wilson, don't you? Sturdy tree of a man. His son Geoff was in your class, first of your classmates to get glasses. You remember that? How you wanted glasses? Chemo cut old Joe Wilson right down. Right down.

You know I can't stay, Ma.

Why do you hate me?

I don't hate you.

At his last summer visit, she microwaved two dinners, and they ate in the living room. She apologized for not vacuuming the area rug.

Looks fine, he said.

The vacuum's so heavy.

He said he could do it.

She said, Guests don't vacuum.

Guests, he thought, didn't have their school pictures taped to the wall. His school pictures stopped at the year he left. He'd never imagined himself as an older man looking at them. If he had, maybe he would have smiled when the photographer told him to.

After dessert, they sat in the backyard in lawn chairs she said she found for a good price at a yard sale.

Pretty sunset, he said.

She agreed.

Eventually, he left.

14

Heza sticks her tongue out at Abe as she leans both arms on the thrift store's display case. She leans forward until her cheek's smashed against the glass, just like Abe's was, and her boots dangle off the floor.

Off the counter, their mother says. How many times do I have to tell you kids? Glass breaks, you'll go right through.

Cut our faces to shreds, Abe says.

Unrecognizable, Heza says.

Disfigured.

Might as well join the circus.

I didn't say that!

Abe and Heza laugh.

Now, Heza.

Heza lowers herself, then walks on a crack in the concrete floor, one toe in front of the other, balancing, arms out.

Did you turn your earrings today? their mother says.

Heza sighs.

Did you?

Yes, Mother.

You can yes-Mother me all you want, but that's what the lady at the store said to do, or they'll get all scabby.

And then your ears will rot off, says Abe.

You wish.

Then people can tell us apart again.

Heza rolls her eyes.

Don't roll your eyes, Heza.

Or you'll see how empty your brain is.

You're full of wisdom and wit today, says Heza.

Abe smiles.

It's the circus, their mother says.

Abe springs up tall on the chair, listening. You hear it?

I mean…their mother says.

You're such a dumb boot, says Heza.

Heza!

Heza shrugs. She always gets in trouble the day the circus arrives. But what kid doesn't? Strung tight as they are, since any moment could be music, honking horns, acrobats springing off the streets like trampolines.

Abe says, Mom won't take you to the circus if you talk to me like that.

Heza says, You're such a dumb boot.

Mom!

This was supposed to be my day off, their mother says, which she says any day she's tired and they're at it again. Most days, then.

Abe begins to worry. Heza's chin is set in *that* way, and his mother's voice has moved from watch to warning. In under a second, their mother could ban them from the circus. Not just for today but all weekend. What if she banned them from every circus from today to death? Could she? Their mother's the all-or-nothing type. As mad and fast as her temper, she could probably ban the whole village from the circus if she wanted.

He shivers.

Any other day, he'd push Heza right into an argument. But not today. He imagines their father lifting off the roof, reaching in, and shaking Heza and their mother by their collars until they stop. At least long enough for the circus to come, then go.

Abe's never met their father but imagines him as a giant. Probably just his father walking into the store would stop their mother and Heza from talking, much less fighting. And if his father appeared, that could mean the circus was here. Their father worked for the circus once, but their mother says he wasn't a real circus man.

Their mother stands beside the display counter and rests her hand on it. Now, I know I don't need to say this, but you stay away from the circus men, you hear?

Abe and Heza sneak looks at each other.

I mean it, their mother says.

It's not like Abe can get pregnant, Heza says.

Abe stares.

Their mother stares.

Just joking, Heza says and twists one of her earrings.

Before their mother loses it, Abe says, Maybe we could run away with the circus this time.

Heza looks at him.

He looks at their mother.

How about it, Mom? Let's run away this year.

Yes! Let's! Heza says. You'll ride the horses, and I'll stick swords through my ears.

Down your throat, Abe says.

I know, but I'd do my ears.

What will Mom be?

Who will you be, Mom?

Raindrops hit against the store windows.

Mom?

But she's gone dark inside.

Kae?

Mom?

Kae?

15

That summer.

When Kae was younger than the acrobats and she stood outside the diner before her shift. She wore her mother's old but best dress, pale yellow and to her knees.

That summer day, the sun tilted above the office building across the street. No lampposts yet, and the hardware store still opened every day at the same time, as did the general store, the lawyer's office, and the realtor who'd come to town to make a go of it, what with the emptying houses.

That summer morning, her first summer working at the diner, Kae waited in front of the diner instead of the back alley where the cooks and waitresses swapped cigarettes, jokes, and silences. They scared her. How the waitresses moved fast. How they cursed. How they laughed suddenly, so loudly, at jokes she didn't recognize as jokes. They had children, husbands, ex-husbands, bills, carpets, and carpet stains that wouldn't come out even with baking soda. Try shaving cream. Oh yeah? Yeah.

The waitresses had plans for the weekend and two cigarettes left in today's pack. Tattooed flowers grew around their wrists, covering names they had once loved. Or maybe it wasn't love in the first place, said the waitresses, sometimes, when the diner was empty and they sat in the last booth rolling silverware into paper napkins.

That summer morning, Kae stood on the sidewalk outside the diner, clutching her blue apron and idly searching the sidewalk for nickels like when she was a kid and her parents were having coffee inside. Back when she thought the waitresses were glamorous because she knew nothing of their lives beyond the diner, or of the world beyond the village.

That's where she was standing that summer morning when the red truck swerved onto the main street and nearly jumped the curb and hit her, taking out her legs and life. The truck came so close that she felt its heat and believed fully in her own death.

Since the moment the truck nearly hit her, she has never been sure whether she did die right then. How could she know? What if death were like standing in the hole of a missing jigsaw piece, while someone else built a continuous puzzle around you?

If she was not hit by the red truck—

If she did not collapse beneath it—

If she was not rushed to the hospital, dying in the ambulance or in the hospital bed once she was tucked into white sheets, white walls, white afternoon coming through the square window—

Then the truck did not hit her.

It swerved just in time. Right up to the curb. Lurching as the driver braked, like an elevator coming to rest.

A boy unfolded from the driver's side and peered at Kae over the roof.

Hey, he said.

She didn't answer.

You think I was gonna hit you? he said.

Kae stared at him. Or the silhouette of him. Hard to see with the light coming from behind him.

Well, I wasn't, he said. I saw you.

She stood still and tried to disappear.

He began to rest his arms on the truck's hood. Then snapped back.

Dammit, he said. Hotter than hell.

She'd heard the joke before, so she knew to laugh.

You're pretty hot yerself, he said.

She blushed and wanted to go into the diner, but felt it would be impolite—even if he had nearly killed her.

I'm not crazy, he said.

Okay.

Or I am, he said.

The passenger door opened and Frank got out. That's when she understood. The red truck, the summer morning, Frank. Circus was coming.

Already? she said.

That's right, said Frank.

You're the last stop, said the Summer Boy.

This *village* is the last stop, said Frank.

The Summer Boy nodded toward the diner. You work here?

You're full of words, Frank said to the boy.

The boy winked at her, then followed Frank around the truck. Frank dropped the tailgate and reached for the box of posters.

Circus will be here in two weeks, said the Summer Boy.

She nodded and felt something shift in her stomach. She'd never been the girl Summer Boys talked to. And now she was. She'd imagined liking it and swooning, like the girls always talked about.

The Summer Boy hauled the long rectangular Tupperware container and set it on the sidewalk. The paste he'd mixed up that morning floated inside it. Frank took out the paint roller. After the truck was packed back up, the Summer Boy handed her one of the posters.

16

Inside the diner, the waitresses gathered around her, looking at the poster, saying, What'd you say? What'd he say? Are you so in love? Was it love at first sight?

She didn't know what to say and so said nothing.

Time, can you believe it?

Time, the way it works.

Thank God the circus is back, said the waitresses and hurried to the kitchen to see the work schedule. The day the circus arrives is the best tipping day of the year.

Is it? she said.

Listen to her.

The best.

So don't think you'll work that day, or if you do get scheduled, you can't have all the shifts. All of us been here longer, and you're a rookie without kids.

No kids—*yet*, another said.

Sooner than later, the way that Summer Boy was looking at her.

Maybe she don't want kids.

What's wanting got to do with kids?

The waitresses laughed and pasted their lives onto hers, then got quiet again as they huddled around the schedule.

17

The circus came, and Kae went and stood in line for a lemon shake-up. She had always loved the moment when it was her turn to peel from the line and approach the shake-up stand window. She liked the size of it and the sound of it sliding open. She liked feeling small against it, standing tiptoe to say her order. She liked how the air in the stand window felt warmer than the summer air, and feeling both. She liked how ordering was like slipping a quarter into an old tin toy bank, automating the lemon shaker to life.

One lemon shake-up, please, she said that summer on the first night of the circus.

The shaker nodded, pulled the towel from his shoulder, and wiped the cutting board clean of the last lemon seeds and pulp. The shaker flipped a couple lemons from a bucket onto the cutting board. The shaker's movements created a breeze that touched her face.

Then a voice behind her said, It's the girl in the yellow dress.

She didn't turn around.

Hey, the voice said.

She focused on watching the shaker. The sound of the ice cubes.

My treat, said the voice, and an arm followed, grazing her shoulder as it reached for the stand's silver counter. She turned. It was the Summer Boy.

I already paid, she said.

I owe you one, he said. For nearly killing you and all.

The lemon shaker handed Kae's shake-up out the window. The Summer Boy took it and sipped from the straw.

That's mine, she said.

NEXT! yelled the shaker.

She'd missed the making of her drink. A whole year she'd waited. Should she order another, or should she go to the end of the line and wait again?

NEXT!

It's good, said the Summer Boy. Wanna try it? he said and held the cup out to her. Around the cup danced cartoonish oranges and lemons on women's legs.

She folded her arms against her chest.

Our turn, said the kids next in line.

Kae mumbled sorry and stepped to the side. She tried to watch the shaker, but watching from this angle wasn't the same.

The Summer Boy offered her the dollar bills in his hand.

She shook her head.

I owe you.

I'm alive, she said.

Maybe that's what I owe you for.

She turned away.

But if you won't take a drink, he said, then I need to pay you for this. He took another drink. Offered it to her again. She kept her arms folded and walked away from the food trucks and stands. He followed. Down the midway, past the tents where men stood by stools, calling out to come see the next show.

You won't believe it!

None like it in all the world!

Sights beyond your wildest imagination!

By the end of the night, the men would be sitting on the stools, rolling back their shoulders for a good stretch. By the next day, they'd sit most of the time, standing only between shows.

But on the first night, there's always that energy that keeps people on their feet.

The Summer Boy walked beside her.

Like you've never seen it before!

The air was hot.

Come on now, come on!

The press of bodies.

The lights.

She began to relax and let her arms swing at her sides.

He slipped his fingers between hers. Her heart jumped.

A clown dropped to one knee and presented a woman the flower from his pocket.

Children ran by, waving plastic swords.

An elephant trumpeted.

The Summer Boy snuck her into a tent where a beautiful man in a tuxedo stood on a stage, lifting doves from his hat.

In another tent stood a woman in a full-length silver leotard, an apple balanced on her head, wrists tied at her back. A man drew an arrow.

Across the way, a woman wore a snake like a scarf, its thick head rising next to her cheek as its tongue flickered and its eyes searched for what snakes search for. A way out? A place in the dark? The memory of itself before the circus?

A man walked by with a lion pelt on his back, its paws bound at his throat. In the way a cape made from a dead lion was a novelty for city crowds, his black skin was a novelty to the villagers.

Of course they'd seen black people on the TV news and in professional sports games.

Of course they'd seen graffiti on the freight trains passing from Chicago to New Orleans and back. Gangs, they said, and shook their heads.

Down the midway Kae and the Summer Boy went, ducking in and out of tents, until they'd reached the last one.

Have you seen Hezada the Great? he said.

Since? she said.

Since, he said.

She hadn't. She'd heard stories, though.

Frank stood outside of Hezada's tent. Frank said, Think again.

Maybe another night, then, said the Summer Boy. Want to see the camp?

She did.

But first he took her back up the midway, pulling her into the biggest tent, around and under the wooden bleachers, the smells of popcorn, sweat, sawdust. Out back of the tent, performers waited, smoking cigarettes, adjusting their costumes, patting their horses. Clowns ran by and into the tent.

The audience cheered.

The lights flashed.

A group of women exited the tent and lifted their feather head-dresses off their heads, and Kae saw the frames that hooked over the women's shoulders. She'd never been so close.

Like two performers done for the night, Kae and the Summer Boy headed back to camp. Performers walked in the distance ahead of them. She thought of the waitresses walking home from the diner after close.

The Summer Boy showed her the clothesline hung with the acrobats' sequined leotards, underwear, nylons.

He pointed at the Strongest Man's camper. He naps between appearances, the Summer Boy told her. And get this, he calls them catnaps.

Doesn't everyone?

But it's the World's *Strongest* Man, he said.

I suppose he'd have to nap a lot.

But *cat*naps? The boy laughed.

In the window of one camper, a woman stood in her underwear in front of a mirror, her back to them. Her shoulder blades made Kae think of a fallen bird. Kae imagined touching the woman's back, how the shoulder blades would feel like frozen waves. They saw each other in the mirror. Peacock feathers sprayed from a vase.

The Summer Boy grabbed Kae's hand and hurried her away.

Where are the elephants? she said.

I'll show you later, he said. That's Frank's camper. He pointed. Now, behind here is me. A small blue tent was raised behind the camper. What do you think? he said.

She didn't think much of the tent, but she thought that everything else was beautiful. The moon, how it pooled on the roofs of the tents. Even the windbreak of trees that would never catch her eye on any other day or night. The distant applause—calling voices—crackling fryers—shaking ice cubes—children crying from exhaustion.

The Summer Boy knelt to unzip the tent.

Come on in, he said. Welcome to my humble abode.

And she followed after him, crawling on her hands and knees.

There was room only for a sleeping bag.

He turned onto his back, an elbow under his head. She turned over too. They looked through a small window in the tent roof. You can see all the way to the moon, he said.

When he kissed her, she tasted the lemonade on his mouth. And then.

And then.

Afterward, she lay there looking at the moon so hard that the mesh covering the window disappeared, the boy disappeared, the stars disappeared like at summer camp when she stared up from her sleeping bag while the snores of the kids around her disappeared.

But she didn't disappear.

Everything about her body felt uncomfortable and wrong. It wasn't at all how the waitresses talked. And they talked sex all the time.

But they'd never mentioned the moon.

Or the sweat.

Or how her thighs felt sealed together.

Or how her bottom felt wet and sticky, or how embarrassed she felt, or how she would use her yellow dress to dry herself, or how awful her stomach would feel.

The circus music stopped like always, and she wished she were at home, in her bedroom, listening through her own window to the crowds walking home, car doors shutting, engines humming into the distance.

But she was here in a Summer Boy's tent being passed by circus performers' voices and shadows.

By now the diner would be closed, and the two remaining waitresses would be washing down the last tables, packing up the salad bar for the night while the dishwashers loaded another rack and the cooks scraped the grills.

It was hot in the tent.

She listened to a group of circus people decide what to do next. I'm tired but I'm not. Yeah.

So it's either have a drink at the village bar or drive to the next town and have a drink there.

Might as well stay here.

They expect us, though. First day in and all that.

That's right. Good for tomorrow's show.

Fuck tomorrow's show.

C'mon.

I mean it. Fuck the circus. That's how I feel.

Why don't you say that louder? Go stand by the circus boss's camper and shout it.

Maybe I will.

Don't encourage him.

Aw, boss is off at his sweetheart's.

The group wandered off.

If they went to the village bar, she knew her father would tell about it tomorrow, as though he were there by coincidence.

She felt along the tent's bottom for the heap of her yellow dress. The Summer Boy had said she could leave it on if she wanted. She found the holes for her arms and head, then crawled out of the tent.

As she stood up, the elephants cried. She remembered the night her father took her onto the porch to listen to them cry.

You hear that? he said.

She did.

18

Frank lifts his foot off the gas.

This is the last curve, the one that makes the meeting of circus and village inevitable.

It's all gravity from here, rolling the camper into the village, followed by the lions and tigers and such, like the magnetic wooden trains he's seen in stores.

Momentum pulls him around the curve.

It's the sort of curve that kills, which is probably what the driver's ed teacher tells every student.

There's the ditch where a small wooden cross stands, wired with blue plastic carnations. Tomorrow or the next night, the parents of this cross may sit under the big top, remembering when their cross was a kiddo who sat between them, rocking and giggling as the spotlights rippled across their legs and hands. Even if the parents of dead children stay home, shut their windows, and blast the air conditioner, the sounds of the circus will creep under the windowsills, press against the siding, taunt out their memories. Because the circus is loud, and death is louder.

It's hard stuff what people go through, Frank thinks.

Circus helps, he thinks.

Maybe.

Maybe just makes things worse.

He never can settle on an answer.

Frank turns off the county road at the far corner of the schoolyard. Red truck's right with him. Good boy. He drops one hand over the other on the steering wheel, like his mother's hands moving over piano keys. He misses watching her play, but her arthritis is bad.

Depressing as hell, she said.

You could try, he said.

You don't know much about my life, she said, not meanly.

The circus sews a path that connects the villages and towns more than maybe even the roads do, or it thickens the roads' connections, maybe. Besides high school sports games, the circus is one of the few things keeping the villages and towns conscious of each other.

It's harder, of course, as soon as another superstore sprouts up and changes the trade routes. Downtowns fray, storefronts empty, and the Dollar Store, the Family Dollar, the Dollar Tree—whatever corporate circuit—moves in, rolls up its yellow BUY ONE/GET ONE posters, and voilà.

Until this is just how it is.

Is what it is.

Isn't it?

People's got to keep living, don't they?

And once a parasite is so dug in, there's no easy way to root it out.

Then what?

19

If Kae hadn't applied at the diner—

Or if it hadn't been her shift—

Or it was her shift, sure, and so she was waiting outside the diner when the red truck killed her—

Or didn't kill her—

Or if she worked at the diner, nearly her shift, she stood on the sidewalk, but she took off that yellow dress? Right there, unbuttoning the three pearl buttons, lifting it above her hips, over her head, just like she often imagined doing in the middle of church—how everyone would gasp and faint while her mother covered her with the church bulletin and rushed her from the sanctuary—

Why would you do a thing like that? her mother would want to know.

I don't know, Kae would say and mean it. This place. This place just.

—Then the Summer Boy would have seen not a girl in a yellow dress but a crowd of people, hauling her and her yellow dress away.

Or maybe he would have simply heard of the girl in the yellow dress, and when he ran into her at the shake-up stand, he would have said, Hey, are you that crazy girl?

That's me! she would have said and taken off her dress again. Ta-da!

Then he would have left her alone. Backed away. Oh, excuse me.

And that would have been that.

The end of the life before it became hers.

Or if she wore the yellow dress, he nearly hit her, but they ran into each other again at the lemon shake-up stand when the circus came. Fine. So then, sure, they walk around the circus field under lights, et cetera, and everything's beautiful, et cetera, and she falls in love with the beauty of it—not in love with him.

But isn't that what did happen?

Okay, but in this version she knows the difference.

But wouldn't she still have followed the moment into his tent? She wanted to know what the waitresses knew, and freedom from that was in that tent. Or so she believed.

And I thought I was in love.

That too.

Did I?

Because she didn't know people could fall in love with a moment.

How could I have?

Now, she'd be more prepared to live her past. Now that she is a mother, mother of twins. Kae who runs a tidy thrift store. Kae with her old dreams. Or, as her children probably imagine, Kae who never dreamed beyond the village, because why else would she still be here?

Probably the twins imagine she's against dreams.

But how can I tell my children my old dreams without their thinking I'm a failure? I may believe it. How can I tell them, especially Heza, that everyone has dreams? It's good to have so many, to fill yourself with them like feathers so that their odds increase.

What thought of the future isn't a dream?

If I hadn't been wearing a yellow dress on a sunlit morning, having arrived early to work.

If I'd been more confident and waited for my shift inside at the counter.

Now, Kae would fill the apron pockets of Kae Past with so many jokes that would make the boys laugh but keep them away.

Kae Now would teach Kae Past how to flirt with everyone so no one could feel special enough to walk her home, or to invite her down the midway, or to allow her to think she was falling in love. But how was the Summer Boy to know she wasn't in love with him when even she believed it?

Did I?

The moment held out a hand. It was dark. The lights of the circus close.

It was beautiful.

Wasn't it?

20

Here's the short row of houses, the green population sign, the school-yard without a school building.

What happened to the school? Frank had asked at the diner. Tornado? Bad electric? Gas line blow, like the one that took out the old KZ Diner?

The men in the diner stared at the old soda fountain covering the wall behind the counter. Its mirror reflected their faces, as did the silver napkin dispensers and glass donut stand, and the mirror reflected those reflections.

Demolished on purpose, one said.

Earlier this year, another said.

Will they build a new one?

Consolidated with the town school now. Probably forever.

Things change.

Nothing lasts forever.

School was there a long time.

You went there, didn't you?

All of us did. My great-great-grandfather went there. There's pictures of him standing on the steps.

I'd like to see those.

A waitress passed behind the counter and said, They auctioned off some of the bricks to raise money.

For what?

To pay for the demolition, maybe.

You buy one of the bricks?

Didn't know what I'd do with it.

Built in the 1800s.

Don't say?

Nah, that was the first school. This school here was the second one. First one burnt in the 1920s.

1917. Was just talking about this the other day. The year my father was born. That's how I remember it.

Helluva man.

Nice of you. Bev found some pictures of him with his graduating class. She might show them at the town library.

I'd like to see that exhibit.

Should.

Should.

Used to be one of those schools for training teachers.

Normal school.

That's right.

One day, Frankie, you'll show up with your circus friends, and there won't be anybody left, way things are looking.

The men lifted their coffee cups to their reflections.

The waitresses cleared dishes from the tables.

21

Most any village graduating class stays the summer until the circus, then leaves for the military or community college. A few go straight to the university. More remain to help on family farms or carpool with their parents to the light-fixture factory, the Hershey factory, the broom, bra, or bagel factory. Others work retail in the university town while waiting for inspiration, true love, or at least the next Friday night.

Kae's senior class was no different. While her best friend went to university four hours north in the Chicago suburbs, Kae lived with her parents and commuted to the community college, which she enjoyed, for the most part, until the second month of classes when she started getting sick. The whole drive, she'd feel nauseated and would pull over to heave into a ditch while trying to stay out of sight of passing cars and trucks.

By the third month, she couldn't make it through a class without leaving for the bathroom. Once she realized she was pregnant, she started imagining that everyone knew too. As she vomited, she imagined that her professor, if not her whole class, every class down the hallway, was listening to her vomit.

They shook their heads. They raised their eyebrows. They exchanged knowing looks. Can you believe it? I mean, really. Who's she trying to kid? Doesn't she have any respect for us trying to learn?

The anxiety worsened until it talked the whole drive to school, interrupted her notes during lectures, showed up while she studied, and eventually doodled in her notebook margins SLUT. SINNER. WANTON.

All words from revivals, Bible stories, myths, rumors of bastard children and shameful women.

Words that a friend had whispered in junior high, on the bus to school; her friend's parents had found out about a boy and sent her to confess in front of the church. At the altar.

In front of everyone.

To tell them what she'd done with a boy in the woods.

Awful, Kae said to her friend.

Her friend shrugged.

Words Kae had read or heard long ago now crept whispering from wherever they'd waited.

By day, it was the anxiety. By night, the dreams came.

She dreamed of walking down the village sidewalk and as people appeared and saw her, they turned to stone. She dreamed of herself floating in an ocean, facing a wide, empty beach surrounded by cliffs. On the beach sat a set of wooden bleachers, and on the bleachers sat soldiers. A helicopter appeared in the gray sky. A bomb dropped. She sang to the soldiers, and some ran into the ocean, trying to swim toward her, still in their boots, laces unraveling, drinking saltwater, becoming confused between ocean and sky. One by one, they drowned, love letters drifting out of their pockets as she swam after them and tugged them to shore.

She wet the bed.

She went whole shifts at the diner without talking.

One day while waiting for a classroom to open, a group of students stood by the door. She felt them whispering about her.

That kind of girl.

She hurried out of the building.

Her professors probably hoped she wouldn't return so they could lecture without interruption.

But wasn't she trying to make a better life for herself?

Even so, why not wait until after the baby? Why drag everyone into her shame?

Should have kept her legs closed.

Shouldn't have gone to the circus.

Shouldn't have worn a dress the color of sunshine.

Can you believe it? Girls like that. And not a ring on her finger.

What's she even thinking, coming to college?

Clearly, she wasn't.

The next day, she stayed home. Her mother felt her forehead. She pleaded a cold and stayed in bed. The next day, she dressed for school, but drove to the creek where she had played as a child. The next day, she made it to class, but a boy stared at her and she imagined him following her, saying hell and abortion, though the nearest clinic was outside the range of the county phonebook as far as she could tell.

Or maybe he'd ask her to the pancake supper, tell her she was making him fall in love with her, and if she'd wait, he'd make an honest woman out of her.

Or maybe he'd slash her throat and dump her at the edge of campus where no one seemed to go.

Or maybe he'd just give her a Gideon Bible or a Bible tract like the man who stood in the middle of the campus shouting, REPENT, SLUTS! at the passing girls until a crowd gathered and security came.

She stayed home the next day.

And the next day, and the next.

She picked up more shifts at the diner.

She threw up and examined the speckles of her vomit.

She grew out of her bras.

22

The village buildings seem etched against the rainy sky. Frank slows the camper. He looks down one sidewalk, then the other.

Tire swings.

Dropped bicycles.

Couches on porches.

A yard statue of a Negro boy running with a lantern to nowhere, repainted white.

Small gardens.

Windsocks.

Mailboxes.

An old woman in a wide-brimmed hat, frowning at her tomatoes.

The curtains twitch in that window. Must be someone trying to peer out while staying hid.

Sky's gone gray. Rain'll be steady by the time they reach the field on the other side of the village. Maybe after the circus wraps up and leaves, Frank will stay here. He'll take his shoes off and walk through the grass gone greener by the rain. Lush green, love green, stay-here-a-while-and-change-your-life green.

Frank's boss once said he's never seen a postcard of a town in the rain, but the way light works in the rain, you'd think every set of postcards would have at least one. In addition to crosswords, the circus boss likes cameras and talking photography when they aren't debating how to keep the circus from going broke without trading the fields for city arenas, like the other circuits. Frank hates the idea of arena circuses.

An air-conditioned circus?

Plush folding seats?

Stairs with aisle numbers painted on them?

Cup holders?

Balloon carts rolling along slick hallways, not even in sight of the action?

Jesus. Floors, even?

Probably there's even a janitorial staff that comes with the rental contract.

Clowns running around on a tarp laid down to protect the polished wooden floors of stadium basketball courts.

I don't like it either, agrees the circus boss. But what if illusion works better indoors now? People don't go outside like they used to.

I don't buy it, Frank says. That's not the circus, that's a musical. A charade. A snow globe.

Just the other day, the circus boss was saying he'd read a piece about how the rich view the world, from way up high in their penthouses and private jets, so high it makes everybody seem so small. Specks. And that's their reality, see? We're not even specks. They've got to imagine us first, even to think of us—that's how small. I doubt they even bother.

Frank shook his head.

What I want to know, said the circus boss, is this. Tell me what you think. Even if they do imagine us, what are we like? What are we like in their imaginations if they can then pretend we don't exist?

Frank said, I'm tired of imagining how other people imagine me.

23

Soon, every kid in the village will appear, running out of their lives and toward the music, like their parents under revival tents.

Is that the circus? Frank says, as though he's peering from a storefront instead of the cracked camper windshield.

That's next week, Frank says.

No, he says, that *sounds* like the circus. Listen.

He flips the music on the loudspeakers wired to the top of his camper.

Sounds like a goddamned ice cream truck, he says.

Since when's there an ice cream truck around here? he answers.

He shakes his head. He glances in the side mirror. Summer Boy's looking out the truck window at sidewalks as empty as every town and village they've seen this summer. This is just the last stop. Maybe the boy's hoping for a welcoming committee for the finale. Foil stars. A ribbon-cutting like the village council had when the lampposts were installed.

Sorry you have to see this, Frank thinks to the Summer Boy, even though every Summer Boy grew up in a place just like this.

Frank's sorry, nonetheless. Not because they're from a place like this—well, maybe a little—but because they have spent most of their lives imagining something so very different beyond the fields and boundaries of their hometown and the surrounding ones, but come to find out what's beyond is just more places exactly like they were trying to imagine themselves out of.

It's a hard realization.

They don't see it early in the summer, of course. But as it turns toward the end, toward autumn, the Summer Boys begin to recognize the pattern of fields, houses, people.

It's a hard pattern to erase once you've seen it.

Hard, even, to watch them see it.

Or hell, maybe it's just Frank who sees it over and over. And he assumes they're seeing it just as he does. Maybe he's the old-timer never content with now. Well, fine. So be it—isn't that what people say?

Now the windshield wipers say So. Be. It.

So. Be. It.

But it makes sense to tell people what life used to be like since you're always seeing that alongside the here and now. Doesn't it?

Maybe he's supposed to pretend he only sees The Now.

Now, the circus is here. The circus, now.

Not that this is a circus, Frank says.

Looks like a circus to me, Frank answers.

Nope. He shakes his head. Not like it used to be. Not like The Circus.

Times are changed, the circus boss likes to say.

Doesn't mean the circus had to.

Oh, c'mon, Frank.

It's not The Circus anymore. Hasn't been The Circus for years.

For one, Frank says, holding his palms over the steering wheel, where's the band? Where's the goddamned band?

Can't think like that.

I know, but.

Frank shakes his head. Can't think like that. Thinking like that kills a person. On the inside, even if the past does run right alongside the present. So it's easy to compare them and decide one's better than the other. Time doesn't feel like it's passing if memory and now seem the same. Is that it?

24

But listen, when the circus had a band, the whole goddamn village came out to greet us—soon as they heard the distant boom-da-boom-boom of the drums. They'd burst from front doors, drop out of windows, rush like fires under wooden sidewalks, all of them coming outside to wait for us to turn this very corner into the center of this very village.

You'd be surprised how far off we'd be and they'd hear us. And wait. They'd wait an hour, maybe more. And waiting's good for business when there's something to wait for. Waiting creeps around your belly and stretches up your throat until you've imagined the band turn this very corner a thousand times before the band actually does, *but* when the band does march into sight, you can't hardly believe your eyes. You're so beside yourself with waiting and excitement and jumping with electricity and drums and the beat, beat, beat of the circus rolling through the downtown, until now you're waiting for that to end, such that every truck and car feels like maybe it's the last, or this passel of clowns, or that herd of horses and women in glittering leotards and bare legs.

Bare legs!

But wait!

Wait?

Yes.

Because now we're rolling out of the downtown and through the park, past the swimming pool where kiddies are shaking the fence and shouting at us. Past the playground where kiddies jump from the swings, tripping, falling, but they dust themselves off and race to the road to wave at us. Past the little bandshell where the village band plays some summer evenings.

Past the baseball field, the horseshoes, the wives waving one hand while pushing strollers with the other.

Everyone waits along the road as we raise the tents. They wait for us to flick on the lights around the ticket booth, the ticket sellers to flip up the blinds and lean forward so you can buy tickets to the first show before it's sold out, but it's always sold out, so you buy tickets for the second, third, fourth show, the whole second day of shows because it's only once a year, the circus, so you buy all the shows, every day of shows, ready to get sick on shows and candy and women unlike the women you know because they're painted, in sequins, up high above everyone, bare feet, bare legs. You haven't waited just hours for the circus, you've waited all fall, all winter, every spring day, hour, second since your life ended when the circus left last summer. Your whole life has been waiting to begin again, and all it takes it a ticket.

One ticket.

Get yourself a ticket to the show!

Aw, it's the same show as last year.

GET YOURSELF A TICKET!

Because anybody who says the circus is the same as always is a fool.

A damn fool!

Canned music don't hold nothing to a big circus band marching up dusty gravel roads, body-weary, grasses clinging to their pants from the fields, music thumping off farmhouse walls and barn doors like a ghost band marching ahead of this band, shaking good china off shelves, vases from tables, salt and pepper shakers off the counter until every wife starts packing her fragiles as soon as the first circus poster appears downtown, and every good wife doesn't unpack them until the last elephant leaves and a day has passed since the last trumpet is heard.

Because there's always a chance, a wish, a hope like the one that makes you watch the sky long after the firework show is over—thinking maybe—just maybe—another firework will sneak up and explode, and you'll be there to see it.

You won't miss it like the rest of the world.

And with the circus, it's the hope that maybe this is the summer the circus won't leave. This time, they'll stay forever. They'll build where the tents stood. They'll lay sidewalks, dig basements.

Impossible!

But just imagine if the circus stays, maybe not forever, but for a year—two years.

Imagine three years of the circus set up in the field, show after show. Snow on the tops of tents. A lion's tracks up a country road. The elephant sitting in the school gymnasium, watching the kids' basketball practices. The circus boss would wear overalls, a baseball hat with the name of a seed company on the front, when he joins the farmers for coffee every morning.

What if we stayed so long the village would be begging us to leave?

Think of it!

Impossible.

But the band.

Those nights with the band.

I'll weep if you make me remember it.

25

After the first semester, many of Kae's former classmates came home for good too. They were getting real about their lives, which is how their parents or grandparents put it as Kae refilled their coffee or cleared their plates.

Like I told him, they'd say, nothing wrong with hard work.

Builds character.

That's right.

Never was much for school to begin with, said one of her classmates when she ran into him in the town grocery.

I don't remember that, she said.

He shrugged. What you been up to? he said.

Oh, you know, she said.

Yeah, he said.

That first Christmas break after university, her best friend came home wearing a new coat and way about her. Though they performed the same rituals, exchanging small gifts, attending the Christmas Eve candlelight service, and scraping together a snowman, it wasn't the same.

The night before her friend returned to university, they walked arm in arm through the village. It was snowing. Each time they circled the downtown sidewalks, Kae imagined saying she was pregnant. Then they'd start the loop again.

How about dinner? said her best friend. My treat.

I'm pregnant, Kae thought. Instead, she said, Sure.

It feels so grown up, doesn't it?

It didn't, really, since she'd worked there nearly a year.

Same as always, Whit said as they approached the diner. The same cardboard Santa waved in the front door's glass. Inside, paper bells hung from the ceiling fan cords. By the cash register stood the artificial tree that Kae helped put together and covered in silver icicles and metallic ball ornaments she had once peered into as a child.

Instead of feeling the usual comfort from the familiar decorations, Kae thought how quaint and cheap they must seem to Whit, who had gifted her a blown glass ornament with the Chicago skyline inside it.

Whit hung up her coat and scarf on the coatrack and chatted about rumors about her next term's classes—how hard the professors were or weren't, who promised to share notes and old tests, why she wasn't too worried.

Kae counted the jellies in the black plastic organizer. It needed refilling.

Most of what we learn, Whit said, nobody needs to know in the real world. But you know.

The real world, Kae said. There were far too many orange marmalades. Someone from another table must have swapped their oranges for grapes.

You know. Like Medieval churches and things like that.

Medieval churches?

Did you have history this semester?

She shook her head. Whit didn't know she'd dropped out.

Here, Whit said and took a napkin from the dispenser and a pen from her purse and started drawing.

Kae listened to the sound of the pen against the table.

Ada came up to take their orders. Thought you were working tonight, she said to Kae.

Guess not.

Lucky duck.

Kae shrugged. I'm still here, right? So not so lucky.

Good point.

I'd like a hot chocolate, Whit said without looking up. Kae noted it.

Whit pushed the napkin across the table.

She needed to get a crib, probably. How long could that wait? Ada had gotten pregnant sophomore year, and Kae had gone to the baby shower in the church basement. If you can go, her mother said, you should go. Not many will. Her mother had been right. It was Ada, Whit, Kae, and Ada's mother and aunts.

Would Ada now attend Kae's baby shower? Does she even want one? Folding tables covered in pink tablecloths and paper-white babies in cardboard bassinets.

Whit pointed at the napkin. This is the nave, she said.

Kae examined the drawing. It looks like a church.

A cathedral.

Kae looked out the window, but the Christmas lights taped to the inside trapped her reflection so all she could see was herself and the room behind her.

Whit crumpled the napkin and smiled.

Ada came with the hot chocolates, took their orders, and left.

So, Whit said, what's up with you?

Oh, you know, Kae said.

You keep saying that, but I don't actually know.

Kae tried to think of anything besides being pregnant.

I met someone, Kae said.

Who? When? I've been home how long and now you're telling me?

The homecoming parade was nice this year.

Oh, no. You tell me about this guy you met. Unless it's a girl.

Kae blushed and shook her head.

Because it's fine if it is.

Hush, Kae whispered.

I'm just saying.

Hush. He was just a Summer Boy.

From the circus? Are you serious? Where was I?

I don't know. You didn't go that night, I guess.

I didn't even know you went.

I went.

Ada pulled the plates from the heat lamp, and Kae busied herself unrolling her silverware.

Ada brought the food, saying, Your parents were in the other day, Whit. Your mother said you were really liking college.

I am, Whit said. How's the kiddo?

Good, good.

How old is she now?

You've only been gone since August, Kae said.

Whit shrugged. I just lost track, I guess.

Davey says Jude's two going on twenty, and it's hard not to agree. Ada laughed.

She's a swell kid, Kae said.

That's great, Whit said. Really great.

They're married now, Kae said.

I know, Whit said.

Beautiful wedding, Kae said.

I so wanted to go, said Whit, and I would have, really, if it hadn't been midterms.

I could show you pictures, Ada offered. They're back at the house.

Whit said, Wish I could, but my train leaves early tomorrow. In about six hours, actually, she said, looking at her watch.

Wait, Ada said. I've got one wedding picture in the car.

Awesome.

Kae watched Ada leave, disappearing into the kitchen where she was parked out back in the alley, probably. She wished she was back there, suddenly.

Awesome? Kae said. Try to mean it next time.

What is with you? I meant it.

She's happy, Kae said and took a bite of her grilled cheese. She felt the burnt lace around the toast shatter between her teeth.

Happy or not, Whit said, she'll never get out of here at this rate.

See, I knew you didn't mean awesome.

Whit blinked. Think about how hard it will be.

Kae took another bite. Last year, she would have agreed. At the beginning of the summer, she would have agreed.

Davey's a nice guy, Kae said. Works hard, watches out for them.

Are you pregnant? Whit said.

Ada came back, snow in her hair and holding a picture. Her cheeks were pink. It's cold out there, she said and set the photo on the table's edge.

It was a picture from the reception of Davey with Jude on his shoulders, dancing with Ada. Jude's in a pink poofy dress, and he's holding her legs while she tugs his ears. All of them balancing, keeping each other upright.

Ada kept the picture behind the steering wheel, covering half the temperature gauge. Kae had memorized it after so many nights driving with Ada after work—around country roads or up the highway to the superstore and its intoxicating aisles.

Funny how it all shakes out.

Kae peered at the window, trying to imagine past the flash of the Christmas lights. Had they been flashing before?

So sweet, Whit said. Where'd you get that dress?

I made it.

It's beautiful.

It was a good wedding, Kae said. A beautiful wedding.

Would have loved to be there. Whit started to hand the picture to Kae.

Oh, Kae's seen it, Ada said. She took it, actually.

Oh, Whit said, still holding it.

Kae shrugged. It was a disposable, she said and drug her last French fry through the ketchup. She licked her fingers one by one.

Ada bought disposable cameras for all the reception tables after reading about it in a grocery store wedding magazine. The idea was that guests would take pictures of the moments at the reception that the bride and groom didn't notice. Candids. Maybe some romantic shots. Turned out to cost a lot to process the film, and of the pictures that developed, most were blurry, badly aimed, or obscene jokes that must have felt funny to whoever took them.

Ada slid the picture into her apron pocket.

Kae traced her fingertip along the brown stripe that circled the plate. A million scratches covered the surface. She moved her head so the light changed, and the scratches seemed to disappear. She straightened her neck, and the scratches returned.

There, not there.

There, not there.

What are you doing? Whit said.

Looking at the scratches that are there, Kae said. Or not there.

You're so weird.

They all laughed. Even Kae, though she hated it when people called her weird.

There, not there.

Whit went to pay and came back with two peanut butter cups from the basket on the counter. They used to beg their parents for them. They still held magic for Whit, but not for Kae, who sometimes refilled the basket and took one or two for herself.

They put on their hats and gloves.

Kae and Ada waved.

See you in the summer, Whit said.

Ada smiled.

Kae and Whit walked into the snowy street. Kae scrunched down in her coat and listened to the snow under her shoes.

So, Whit said. Are you?

Am I what? Pregnant?

No, are you going to live here forever, or what? Whit said.

It's not so bad, Kae said.

They turned toward their neighborhood. Most of the front yards held blow molds of plastic snowmen and nativity scenes. A few yards boasted larger-than-life inflatables. Fewer homes decorated minimally, with a front-door wreath or electric candles in the windows.

What about that boy?

Just a Summer Boy.

Maybe he'll come back in the summer, Whit said.

Maybe.

She had a job. Her parents would disown her or help her. Maybe they already knew but were waiting for her to say it, or maybe they hoped that one day soon, she'd fit in the yellow dress again, and then nobody would have to say anything.

Snow fell on the quiet streets.

When I graduate, Whit said, I'll come back here and we'll live in a little house.

That old dream.

Will you visit me? Whit said.

Kae laughed.

What?

Sure, Kae said.

Why'd you laugh? Whit seemed hurt.

I'll visit. I'll meet all your friends. It will be great.

It's lonely without you, Whit said.

Yeah, Kae said. Same here.

They took each other's hands and squeezed gently before turning away toward childhood homes that weren't quite theirs anymore. Kae watched Whit open the front door, then disappear behind it.

Kae walked on. She felt bright with energy and walked past her parents' house instead of going in. Behind the picture window, her mother worked a jigsaw puzzle on the card table. Probably white sheep on a green hill crossed by old stone walls. Her mother liked that faraway sort of picture. Her father was probably in the recliner, feet up. The TV was on.

She walked on. There was also the joy she felt about being pregnant. She had started feeling calmer and, often, even happy. But she couldn't tell anyone. She wasn't supposed to be pregnant in the first place, much less look forward to meeting the baby.

She walked to the end of the street and into the park. Most of the time, the park's empty. Maybe someone eats lunch in the picnic shelter, or in their truck. Maybe a parent sits near the merry-go-round while a few kiddies turn on it or swing from the old carousel horses. It felt less empty in the snow. Even the orange lights looking into the park seemed busy with the flurries.

She walked around the swimming pool, drained until summer. She approached the fence, looking in. She let the weight of her body lean against the wires. She'd have the baby before the pool opened again. Maybe this summer she'd bring the baby, sit on the edge of the kiddie's section, and hold her daughter between her knees, the water tickling the bottom of her feet. That would be nice.

There's the bandshell where the town band played on summer nights; she and Whit twirled with the fireflies while parents watched from lawn chairs or cars, clapping or honking after each song.

There's the batting cage where Jay went every night after he came home from the war. You could hear his bat hitting the ball from nearly anywhere in the village. Over and over. Then he moved to Florida. Good for him.

She walked through the picnic shelter. She looked up into the rafters for the hook where the DJ's portable disco ball spins on homecoming nights when the picnic tables get moved into the grass, and the kids dance, and the parents visit in small groups. Some of the retirees dance, but always as though they're making fun of themselves for enjoying it. The DJ's disco ball turns, speckling everyone with colored lights. On slow songs, a few older kids dance, shifting from foot to foot, arms around each other's necks and waists. She'll bring the baby to see the lights. We'll try to catch the speckles in our fists. We'll try to trap the colored lights on each other's cheeks. We'll giggle into each other's faces.

The trees held the shape of her childhood in their branches. The snow fell on the play equipment under the orange park lights, so it seemed like the skeletons of large creatures left in a frozen tundra. She stood there for a long time.

26

Remember the nights.

After the show closes and the audience has wandered home. Now the band gets a-going, no matter how blown through they are, but carrying on through midnight until the mayor's walking up the midway in his bathrobe and slippers, shaking his fists and threatening to throw everybody out. This is people's homes. People's got to work in the morning. *You*'ve got work in the morning. Wrap it up, friends.

Sorry about that, Mayor. Sir Mayor.

Have a drink, Sir Mayor?

Why you keep calling me that?

I don't know your name, Sir Mayor.

That's not my name.

Well, it's not my name either.

Everybody so drunk it's funny. Leo on the upright bass plucks the punchline off a string.

More laughter.

A drink for your trouble, Mayor.

A drink will help you get back to sleep.

No such thing as The Circus without The Band.

27

We can't afford a band, his boss said.

Then we can't afford a circus, Frank said.

I'm not saying that. But it's not untrue.

We can't *not* afford a band.

It'd been a raw fight between Frank and his boss the day they scrapped the band, which was down to five guys by then. Can't even call it a band, his boss said.

And Frank knew it, but these five guys had once been five of thirty guys. Five of fifty. Five of a hundred if Frank believes his childhood memories of the circus parading up the streets of his own town while he watched from the curb. After the band came the smallest husband and wife in a heart-shaped wicker carriage pulled by six small dogs. The man waved his top hat. The woman waved a handkerchief. Frank waved back with both hands.

When Frank ran away from town, or ran toward the circus, the couple no longer worked there, having moved to Hollywood. He learned that they'd never been married. Or in love. In fact, said Hezada, he was kind of a dick. But, what's new? I'd be a dick, too, if I had to be a sweetheart all the time.

Sometimes you are, Frank said.

Touché, said Hezada.

When the circus boss let go of the remaining five musicians, they weren't surprised. They'd been planning their what's-next. Cruise ships. Hotel lounges. Travelling Broadway shows. Casinos on rivers, reservations. A few felt too old to gig and figured the women they once loved might be divorced or widowed, or at least available for a drink, a memory or two.

One trumpeter stayed on a while after the others left, helping where he could, but one morning he was gone too.

Frank wept alone. How alone he felt.

Fuck you, fuck you, says Frank with the windshield wipers.

He turns up the speaker volume until the speakers are rattling his bones and nobody can hear him cursing over the music.

Fuck you, fuck you.

28

On the porch of one house, a child pops up from an overstuffed chair. Like a mole or squirrel. He rubs his eyes. He blinks. His hair's mussed. His clothes wrinkled. The child looks side to side. Now he's squinting at Frank and reading the name of the circus of the side of the camper.

The kid reads it again.

Kid's eyes narrow. Then widen.

Hezada! the kid yells, and in one strangely beautiful motion, the kid leaps from the chair, off the sagging porch into the yard, and into a tangle of bicycles. He's all arms and legs, nearly falling as he rights himself, but catches his balance. Now he's running. Across the yard, onto the sidewalk.

Hezada! Hezada! he's yelling and chasing Frank.

Hezada! the kid's still yelling. Hezada! Hezada! Cupping his mouth and swinging his head from side to side, throwing his voice onto yards like yesterday's paper come late.

Frank laughs. He waves. Then he hangs his arm out the window and presses his fingertips against the outside of the door like it's strung with guitar strings, though he can play only a few chords. Which embarrasses him, but he doesn't know why. Maybe because after the first time he tried to run away, his mother asked how he could run away to the circus without a talent.

I have a talent, he said.

Oh yeah?

He shrugged.

You play violin? Fiddle?

He shook his head.

You tap dance?

He shook his head.

What about magic? You got any of that?

He didn't, and of course she knew it.

How will you support yourself? It's not enough to be you, she said.

There's others like me there.

In what way.

You know.

It's not enough, his mother said, unless you want to be played a fool.

They're not fools, Frank said. If they are, I am.

You're my baby, she said. Always will be. But to be in the circus without a talent is to be played a fool.

You don't understand, he said.

I can teach you piano. We can start where we left off.

No. He liked the mystery when he listened to her play. He didn't want to think about the piano as she played it. He just wanted to hear it.

What will you do?

I'll get by.

What's this about, baby? You don't even like the circus.

It was true. But the more she tried to help him, the more he felt his heart break.

29

Here come more children. Around corners, from both ends of the street.

Noisemakers on bicycle spokes.

Skateboards bum-bumping over sidewalk cracks.

Several kids emerge from the recessed doorways of the brick buildings where they live upstairs.

There's Jude, Heza says, looking out the thrift store window.

Hurry up, she says. She pushes and pulls the door. The bells jangle.

I am, I am, Abe says. He's balancing the crutch on his shoulder and trying to mount the skateboard.

Abe! It's *here!* says Heza, jangling the door harder.

I *know*!

She groans.

He groans back.

She steps outside but holds the door for him.

He grabs for the handle and pulls himself forward. The skateboard wheels jam at the threshold.

Give me a push, maybe, he says.

Heza lets go of the door. It knocks against the skateboard, and he jumps off to keep from falling.

Heza's crossing the sidewalk.

Mom! Abe yells.

Heza's hurrying across the street in the red boots.

Mother!

But their Mom's in the back, sorting donations with the radio on.

Even if she does hear him or Heza or the circus, she'll pretend not to. Or ignore it all. Whatever it takes to get her way. That's what her last boyfriend said, with such conviction that Abe believed it. Heza didn't. But Heza doesn't like anyone their mother dates. Mom's just always smarter than them. Abe asked why, then, Mom acts like the boyfriends are smarter.

Because that's how women do, Heza said.

Do you?

Heza shrugged.

Now, Heza's on the opposite sidewalk.

Wait up!

She's not looking back.

Hey!

He uses the crutch to ferry himself across the sidewalk and into the street.

Heza's climbing into the doorway and onto the landing where her friend Jude stands. Jude lives with her mom upstairs above the diner. Their moms are friends from way back. Jude holds three tennis balls behind her back. She taught herself how to juggle last summer by watching countless internet videos of people juggling in their living rooms, backyards, one on a beach, several on pallet stages. More than one had organ grinder music edited in.

Jude peeks around the doorframe and up the street. Usually, the jugglers are near the front of the caravan, but she can't see the caravan yet, only hear the circus music playing out of Frank's camper speakers.

She can wait. Heza will wait with her. And Abe, probably. Her father will pick her up tonight, and she'll stay the weekend with him. He bought the tickets when she called to tell him the posters had arrived.

The circus is coming! she told him.

On my way, Judy Blue! he said. And he left work early to drive to the town where the circus was already performing so he could buy tickets in advance.

Then, that whole weekend Jude had visited him, he teased her by pulling the circus tickets from his back pocket, from behind her ear, from his sleeve, the tablecloth, the toaster, beneath the bathroom door while she was brushing her teeth.

How they laughed and laughed! It was a great joke, and she loved him.

Of course, he'd been the first she showed her juggling to.

That's real good, he said. And he'd clapped. Should you bow? he said.

I dropped one, she said.

That's okay, he said. You bow no matter what.

Okay, she said. Then bowed.

They smiled at each other.

You taught yourself something, he said. That's so cool. He shook his head in amazement and hugged her. That was a good weekend too. Every weekend they're together is good.

30

It's really raining now, Jude says.

Heza frowns at the sky and squints to keep the raindrops from her eyes.

Did it rain last year when the circus came?

No. Yes. Can't remember.

It didn't, says Abe as he rolls into the curb.

You focus on you, Heza says.

He's trying to jump the curb.

It's not going to work, Heza says.

He ignores Heza, pushes himself back, and rams into the curb again.

You need momentum, says Heza.

You're momentum, he says. He brushes his knees off.

She shrugs.

Jude shrugs.

Paint cracks and peels all around the doorframe of the entryway where they stand. It's chipped worse where Jude's picked at it while her mother and the new boyfriend argue. Heza has picked at it too, while waiting for Jude to wake up and come play. Abe too, while waiting for Heza and Jude to decide whether they'll let him play.

You going swimming after the circus gets here? Jude says.

We're going now, Abe says, so we can see it from way up.

That right? Jude says.

Heza shrugs. Maybe. You?

No way, says Jude. I don't want to be there if Mom shows up at the pool like last year. Carrying a ratty bath towel and wearing one of her high school bikinis, elastic shot and sagging. Like she don't know the circus men just got there. No, thank you. No, ma'am.

Jude turns away, then back. She pushes her chest out and presses her hands against her hips. She's got two tennis balls stuck up her shirt.

Look at me, Jude says, raising her voice in the way she does when she's pretending to be her mother.

Heza feels like she's stepped into a pond that's been in the sun all day. She looks away. At her feet. At the thrift store window; hopefully her mother's not watching. Her mother seems to see everything even when she's not watching.

Yoo-hoo! Jude says.

Heza looks. It's just a joke, she tells herself. Just laugh. Laugh.

Heza laughs.

Abe smiles, then drops the skateboard. He sets a foot on it and rolls it back and forth. He wants to stand out of the rain with the girls, but Heza will make a fuss, and he doesn't want Jude to see that. If the rain gets harder, they'll let him in, probably. He'll just have to wait.

Where'd you get that crutch? Jude says.

Somebody dropped it off yesterday, Heza says.

She didn't ask you, Abe says.

Well?

Somebody dropped it off yesterday, Abe says.

Cool, Jude says.

You wanna try it? he says and pushes himself up to the doorway.

Maybe, Jude says.

Circus will be here any minute, Heza says. Right, Abe?

He nods. I got one of the posters in my bedroom, he says to Jude.

Which is stealing, Heza says.

Everybody's got one.

I don't, Heza says.

Abe says, Only because you were busy getting girly-girl earrings.

I like your earrings, says Jude.

Your hair's good too, says Abe. He shrugs. Besides, Abe says, if the posters ain't for sale, it can't be stealing.

Don't say ain't.

I'm right, ain't I?

You can't take a statue out of somebody's yard, can you? That's not for sale.

That's different.

How?

Heza rubs her head. She can feel the water droplets sitting on her head, in her hair. Didn't used to feel that. Probably they rolled off like they do Jude's longer hair.

It's closer, Heza says.

They listen. It's true.

Maybe, Abe says, they'll stay the whole rest of the year until next summer, and then they won't have to arrive because they'll already be here.

The girls look at him.

It could happen, he says.

But then there wouldn't be posters.

True. Well. Maybe they'd print some up anyway for when they plan on performing.

If they stay, they might not perform ever again.

Why's that?

Well, they'd be like us, and we don't perform.

They could teach us how. We could switch places. Villagers could perform for the circus.

The rain falls.

Heza twists her earring in her ear.

31

When Heza asked her mother for short hair, her mother said, How short?

Heza pinched her fingers together.

People will think you're a boy.

Nothing wrong with being a boy, Heza said.

I know. I mean…

Girls can have short hair, Heza said.

Yes.

Abe and I basically have the same face, and he has short hair.

That's true, said her mother. Her mother made arguing hard because she often agreed with Heza's reasoning but not her conclusions.

Lots of women movie stars got real short hair.

We don't live in Hollywood, her mother said.

So if we lived in Hollywood, I could have short hair.

Sure.

Heza groaned.

Not my rules, kid.

Where do you even get these rules?

Her mother shrugged. The village air, I guess.

Well, stop breathing it.

Her mother laughed, though her face didn't.

I could cut my hair myself, Heza said. Or Jude could do it.

You could, said her mother.

Why can't I have short hair?

You can. But I don't agree with it. It's not so safe around here, and what's my job as your mother?

To keep us safe.

That's right. And as your mother, I advise you to delay having Hollywood hair until you're living in Hollywood, or at least until you're older.

Is the world really so much better when you're older?

Her mother paused. In some ways.

Not through and through?

Why would it be?

Heza shrugged. You think someone would hurt me for having short hair?

I don't know, her mother said.

After a few days of thinking how to convince her mother about the short hair, Heza asked about getting earrings in exchange for short hair.

Her mother didn't immediately say no.

Earrings are girly, Heza said.

Girly isn't the goal, Heza. I'm just trying to protect you.

From what?

Ideas, I guess. People who have different ones than you and I do. It's irritating, but you'll have to trust me, I guess. I could be wrong. Maybe little girls with very short hair don't get it as badly as I would have when I was a kid. I'm just concerned, Heza.

Get it?

It's a saying.

Get what, though?

Bad things, Heza.

Like pregnant?

Her mother sighed. Pregnant isn't always bad.

You just say that because you think it hurts our feelings that you got pregnant by accident.

Oh, Heza.

But I'm right that earrings would help, right? Right?

Do you even want earrings?

No, but I want short hair.

And that's worth holes in your ears?

I don't know, Heza said. Maybe?

I guess you couldn't know, her mother said. Can I think about it?

32

They drove the hour to the jewelry store in the Mattoon mall to get Heza's ears pierced. The store was dipped in pink and hung with thousands of earrings and necklaces and rows of sequined purses for prom. The store lady smelled of perfume and led Heza to the counter and a see-through plastic stool. The store lady's name hung around her neck on a lanyard that brushed Heza's knuckles as she leaned in. She slipped Heza's earlobe into the piercing gun.

Will it hurt?

Everybody's different, she said, then pulled the trigger.

It hurt. Waves of heat moved through her the rest of the day. Her mother apologized by taking her to a movie. Then to have her hair cut.

How Heza loves her new hair, or the removal of her old hair. Whatever it is, she enjoys how much lighter her head feels now. One day, she'll shave her head to the skin like her mother shaves her legs. How will she feel then? How free can she be?

33

The apartment door opens at the top of the stairs.

You down there, baby? calls Jude's mother, Ada.

Jude doesn't turn to look.

Every stair's rotted in some place, every board faded to gray. Ada is silhouetted in the apartment doorframe. Her legs are bare, and she wears a flannel shirt that's too big for her, the wrists rolled and the hem hanging to mid-thigh. It's probably her last or newest boyfriend's shirt. They all look the same, the flannels or the boyfriends. The mothers think so too, and wonder whether they're swapping boyfriends like they once swapped candy necklaces for lollipop rings. You might like this one better. Thanks, I'll try it. Any luck? Nope. Too bad. It is what it is.

Heza elbows Jude.

Jude presses against the doorframe.

I see you, Ada calls down. That you, too, Heza? Abe?

It's me, says Heza. She looks up the dark stairway.

You kids hear that racket? Jude's mother calls.

It's the circus, Heza calls back.

No way.

Yeah, way.

Already?

Yep.

Serious?

Serious as serious.

How far away?

Real close.

You don't say.

Yep.

Ada shifts from foot to foot, the light peering over one shoulder, then the other. You kids wanna watch from up here? Pretty good view.

No way, Jude whispers.

She's being nice, Heza whispers.

I do, Abe says, immediately seeing how much higher than the diving board it would be.

Ada is right that it's a good view from the apartment's floor-to-ceiling windows, which frame the whole of Main Street. You'd never imagine how beautiful the apartments are in the buildings. Everyone who sees the windows for the first time says, Jesus, don't tell anybody about this. What's your rent, again? Jesus, yeah, can't let word get out about a view like this.

It's not like the apartment's looking out on Indy or Chicago.

Think if it were. Man, oh man. A view like this? We'd never see it. I'll tell you that much.

Hell, maybe you *should* let people know. Sell tickets to the sunset.

There's an idea. Or tickets to the fireworks. I bet you can see them coming up in three different towns.

You can, actually.

Damn.

Heza looks at Jude. You want to?

Jude shakes her head.

Abe's oblivious, one arm hooked around a lamppost as he rolls around it. His head's tipped back and his mouth's open for raindrops.

Heza wonders whether it's acid rain, but she can't remember if it's acid rain or global warming that's real, or both, or…

Maybe later, Jude calls up to her mother.

Circus only passes through once, Ada says.

I'm being polite, says Jude. We don't want to watch it up there, Ada.

What's wrong with up here? And I'm your mom, not your Ada.

It stinks like man, for one, Jude whispers.

Heza bites her lip to keep from laughing.

What?

Nothing, Jude says.

I'd watch my tone if I were you, girl, Ada says.

Heza rubs her hand up the nape of her neck and over her head. The touch feels reassuring. The first time Jude saw the haircut, she rubbed her hands on it. Is it lucky like a rabbit's foot? Jude asked her. Heza said maybe and tried to feel but conceal the fireworks going off inside her.

I mean it, Jude's mother is saying.

I know, Jude says.

Then act like it.

What's that even mean? Jude whispers.

Heza shrugs a little, so Jude can feel it but Ada can't see.

Why don't you go out on the sidewalk to watch?

It's raining, Jude calls up.

Tone, Jude. Tone.

Ada, it's raining. You said you couldn't hear, so I had to say it louder.

Mom, corrects Ada. *Mom*, it's raining. Try again.

Mom, Jude says, it's raining.

Ada taps her fingernails against the light-switch plate, deciding whether to pursue the argument. Her boyfriend's snoring in the background. He promised to leave before she woke up. So she gave in. But they never understand, or pretend not to. Every one of them got some excuse about why they can't leave. Because she's the love of their life. Because their childhood gave them troubles but hers somehow didn't. How much of falling in love is taking on their troubles? Too much.

When it's done raining, she calls down to Jude, we'll go buy tickets for the first show.

Dad's taking me, Jude says.

Is he?

He bought tickets as soon as the posters came.

That's right. Did he get one for me?

Why? Jude says.

Because I carried you in my womb for ten years.

Jude rolls her eyes.

Her mother laughs.

Heza smiles.

Abe's drinking rain.

Jude rubs her thumb against a tennis ball. She bounces one off the wooden planks of the entryway, then catches it. She bounces another. Then another. The floor has a hollow sound. Dirt or something under there. The tennis balls return again and again to the cup of Jude's hands.

34

The nose of Frank's camper appears around the corner of the old hardware store.

There! Abe says, lifting his crutch to point.

Jude and Heza rush onto the sidewalk. They straighten their backs and link elbows like they've been practicing. They lift their knees and march into the street. The rain flicks off their eyelashes, their foreheads, their cheeks. Abe rows the skateboard alongside them.

Now! Abe shouts, raising the crutch like a conductor's baton. The girls march forward, ushering the circus in.

35

Are we there yet? says a voice from behind Frank.

Thought you'd sleep through it, Frank says.

Tried to, says the man who climbs from the back of the camper and into the passenger seat. Frank glances over. Everything about the circus boss seems heavy and wrinkled.

The boss squints out the windshield. There's no sunshine, but the sky's that bright gray.

Raining.

Yep.

What's this? says the boss, nodding toward the kids. One's on a skateboard and using a crutch. The crutch's arm cushion has a red rag duct-taped around it.

Welcome Committee, I guess, Frank says.

He scratches his chest, watching the two girls marching out ahead of them.

They've been practicing, he says.

Looks like it.

The boss reaches between the seats for his camera bag. He breathes heavily as he lifts it to his lap and unzips it. He pushes back the yellow squares of foam he cut to fit the bag and protect the camera and lenses. He lifts the camera to his eye. Removes the lens cap. Frames up the children. He holds his breath as his finger hovers over the shutter button. The girls lift their right knees, Jude's worn-out sneakers, Heza's red boots. He exhales heavily.

Light seems good, Frank says as he leans back against the seat.

Not too bad, the boss says, examining the camera's screen. The camera beeps as he scrolls back through the pictures from last night. You ever seen somebody die?

Frank shakes his head.

Not just the dying part, but the very end?

Not yet, Frank says. But I've been in love. How is she?

She's dying.

And how is that?

He shakes his head. I don't know how that is.

How's she? Frank says.

Still her, somehow. Thinner. Gave her your regards. She wanted me to take her picture.

Did you? Frank says.

Yeah.

Hard stuff.

Yeah.

She didn't want to see it, though.

Frank nods. He doesn't want to see the pictures either, and the boss doesn't offer to show him.

She won't be here next summer, the boss says. Maybe won't even make it to winter.

The boss rests the camera on his lap and looks out the passenger window. Posters are gone, he says.

Kids started taking them before we'd left.

Good. That's good. The boss rolls down the window. He rests his hand over his mouth like he does when he's thinking.

The boss shrugs and looks out at the empty storefronts, the FOR SALE signs, their reflections passing as ghosts must.

Maybe I'll fall in love again, right?

Frank doesn't say.

She won't, though.

No, Frank says.

The boss raises the camera again, aiming at the brick buildings still lined with last year's Christmas lights, glass bulbs filled with gray sky. He wonders if he should feel superstitious about photographs of the empty village following the photographs of his dying sweetheart. To see her like that and somehow have memories of when she wasn't like that. How to hold both?

Maybe he'll fall in love. Maybe Frank will too. Isn't that the hope that rolls them down to Florida and keeps them waiting all winter? Hope for the sort of love they've felt two, maybe three times—love that will free them from mending costumes, walking tightropes strung across beaches, assuring fused twins, lobotomized mothers, alcoholic fathers that audiences aren't paying to laugh at them, they're paying to forget their lives, and when they do, they start laughing.

But is that true?

It's hard to know what the audiences believe. What has buying a circus ticket ever meant?

Has it simply always been the job of the circus to make all their guests feel like tourists?

Is the village the host, or is the circus?

But love. Now love, that's something that can make spring change its meaning from time to leave, to time to stay.

36

This is where the band stopped, Frank says.

Don't start that again.

You remember it. The sudden silence would strike everybody. Everybody gone still for a second. And then, one drum. Then the next.

Frank.

Then the whole line of them going.

We couldn't keep the band.

Fuck if we couldn't, Frank says.

The boss laughs. Better to think about that than death or your girl's death. Just for a bit.

Frank pulls the camper into its reflection on the diner window and parks.

37

HEZADA is painted across the side of the small camper. A few of the letters are embellished with silver sparkles, like they're so damn shiny.

HEZADA. The people inside the diner read HEZADA over and over until they realize what it means. Then they stand, trying to see beyond the camper blocking the diner window and view.

HEZADA.

They lean this way, that way.

HEZADA.

They stand up taller.

HEZADA.

And taller—rising onto the balls of their feet—flip-flops slapping the floor.

HEZADA.

They touch the table or booth for balance, until there's only giving up. Frank's camper is too much in the way, so they carry their coffee mugs and platters of pancakes, biscuits and gravy, ham and cheese omelets out of the diner and onto the sidewalk.

It's raining hard now, so they try to stay under the diner awning, or under the hanging petunias, or under the concrete ledges of the second-floor windowsills above them. Excitement pulls a few to the edge of the curb. One man steps into the street and looks down it.

38

More kids are coming up the alley on bicycles, skateboards, scooters. A few jog along, shouting to slow down.

Is it terrorists? one child says to another, breathlessly.

Can't tell.

You bet it's terrorists. You bet your sweet mother that terrorists is exactly what it is.

Terrorists? one of the youngest asks.

Better than terrorists.

What could be better? The children have no idea. Well, they pretend to have no idea. They've lived here their whole lives, of course. They stand on their pedals, trying to see. They crouch forward. They pedal harder. The bikes sway under them. They stand again, coasting.

Terrorist! shouts a child pedaling fast.

The kid's pedaling so fast he swerves against the alley wall, scraping his arm as he brakes.

Terrorist! he shouts again and rolls off his bike to the ground.

Frank pauses where he stands behind the camper.

Heza and Jude turn to look.

The boy reaches over his shoulder for the toy assault gun he got for his birthday. Broken glass scatters the alley like rain. He pulls himself forward on his elbows and knees, trying to stay low. It's easier in his backyard, but this is what he's been training for. The real deal, Lucille, as his uncle says.

The boy with the gun shuts one eye and peers through the scope. He takes a breath. The alley smells of hot asphalt and dumpster.

This is it, he thinks.

Wait! shouts the leader. She's throwing up her arm and braking so the other kids brake too. Their tires skid, and they lock their elbows to keep their handlebars from jackknifing their bikes to the ground.

The boy with the gun reaches into his shirt for the plastic spyglass he got in the mail. He kisses the spyglass like the sniper in his favorite war movie. He examines the smeary print of his lips on the plastic before dropping the lens back down his shirt.

The girl on the lead bike has climbed off and is unbuckling her helmet. She holds up one hand to keep the rest of the kids in the alley.

Stop! she shouts.

The boy with the gun jumps to his feet and takes off running, sliding off balance as he bursts from the alley, yelling. He aims the gun at Frank.

Watch out!

Frank!

Frank turns.

The boy's yelling bloody hell.

Frank stretches out his arm and aims his finger at the boy. He cocks his thumb.

Goddamn you! the boy's yelling and aims the gun at Frank's chest.

The boss turns off the circus music.

All is quiet and heat.

The boy pulls the trigger as Frank triggers his index finger.

There's the plastic sound of whirring beads moving through the plastic gun, invisibly piercing Frank's body. Frank drops his arm, his invisible gun twirling around the street and into the gutter.

The diners gasp.

Frank falls back, arms out, as his body crumples to the street. First, he crosses his eyes. Then he rolls his eyes toward the sky.

Everyone watches Frank's chest for its final breath.

The children hurry out of the alley. They hold their faces. They clap.

Frank raises his head. He winks at them.

They scream in fear and delight.

Then he lets his head fall again, tongue lolling from his mouth.

Christ Jesus! The circus has come to town.

39

Frank's dead in the street.

The boy with the gun sits on a curb with his head down, arms dangling over his knees. He never wanted to move to this place. Didn't he tell his mother? Didn't he cry hard as he could?

His mother said they couldn't afford summer day care, so this is the plan. If your father were alive, things would be different, trust me.

If Dad were alive, he wouldn't want to live here.

Pretty sure he'd only care about living, said his mother.

And that was that.

His mother grew up in the village, and his aunt still lives here with her farmer husband. For now, they live with them. His aunt's alright. She collects glass animals and lines them up on the window-sill, and it's an old house, so you have to walk carefully or a glass crocodile will fall and break its tail. Maybe they'll move back. After his birthday. Or after Christmas.

But man, oh man, he hates this place. That's what his father used to say. Man, oh man. The boy shakes his head like his father would. Man, oh man.

Fresh air's good for you, his mother says. More freedom too. Run around town all day without a babysitter. That's fun, right?

Air's hot and he just killed a man with a toy gun that maybe isn't a toy after all. Or it was a toy gun until he aimed it at the man. It's unclear how magic works.

The plastic spyglass swings from the boy's neck, moving a dot of light back and forth on the street between his shoes. It's the sun. Or refraction. One of those words.

He's scared to look up, what he'll see. Blood pooling under the man. A circus man, no less.

Not a terrorist, you idiot, one of the kids said, hitting him upside the back of his head.

That's Frank, you moron.

Who's Frank?

Frank! Frank's Frank! That's who Frank is!

And now Frank's dead, and I shot him. With magic. His stomach hurts.

Don't vomit, he thinks.

Might make you feel better, he thinks in his father's voice. His father vomited a lot toward the end.

He taps the plastic lens with his finger to send it moving again.

That's a good boy, his father would say. Focus on that and nothing else.

So he does.

A kid in red shorts and a yellow tank top picks up the murder weapon from the curb with two fingers like a TV detective and carries it back to the others. The others lean in, trying not to breathe on it, unsure how DNA works, if theirs is on it now and they could be tried for the crime.

Looks plastic, one says.

Sure does.

Don't point it at me, says another.

It's a fake.

How'd it kill him, then?

They turn to look again at the man dead in the street.

Try it, says one.

Get your fingerprints on it, if you do.

It's just a toy.

He's dead, ain't he?

Should somebody call 9-1-1?

Someone at the diner probably has.

Give it here, says a kid in corduroy pants rolled twice. He slips his finger around the trigger and lifts the gun to his shoulder. The others take a breath. He points it at one alley wall. The kids step back. He pulls the trigger. The gun pop-pop-pops as plastic bullets roll through it.

The murdering boy covers his ears and presses his forehead against his knees.

A few jump back. The rest drop into crouches, heads down, balling up like they do during active shooter drills at school.

The gun goes quiet.

Nothing, says one, examining the wall.

Nothing, says another who washes her palm across the brick, feeling for bullet holes like the building in Chicago where people tried killing Al Capone. Her parents took a family picture on the steps. All of them grinning while she points at a bullet's indention in the wall. Is it too grim to use this for Christmas cards? her mother wanted to know.

40

Heza stands over Frank. Her head blocks the rain from his face.

How long you gonna be dead? she says.

He squints one eye up at her. Decade ago, it could have been her mother's eyes he'd have been peering into. That yellow dress.

Heza moves a little, and rain drops on his face and throat. She moves back. She counts the beauty marks under his left eye. Three.

They still watching? he says, clearly trying not to move his mouth.

She starts to look.

Don't look, he says.

How'm I supposed to do that? she says.

He doesn't answer.

She tries to look but not look. Hurts her head.

Maybe he didn't hear her. Maybe she should say it again, louder. Probably she'll get in trouble when her mother finds out she's talking to a circus man. Even if it is Frank. Frank either doesn't count or counts twice as worse, depending on her mother's mood and if her mother's watching right now from the thrift store window. Heza looks across the street, but the light's angling in a way that even if her mother's standing right there on the other side of the glass, Heza can't see her.

Heza looks at the boy on the curb, the girl washing her palm over the side of the wall.

Sort of watching, Heza says through her teeth to Frank.

Frank slides his sunglasses back over his eyes. The lenses are scratched to hell, but turn her into two of herself looking back at her.

Must be what her mother means when she says the thing about

circus men is they always make two of you, and this new you, this second you, they convince you into thinking is the real you. But it's a trick. Remember that. You don't like to be tricked, do you? You don't want to be the sort of girl who falls for that trick, do you?

No.

I fell for that trick.

Yes, Mother.

But you won't.

No.

No matter how beautiful the circus looks, it's a trick, and you'll see it, right?

Right.

Be the you that you are, not the you that you wish to be.

Seems hard.

It is.

Frank raises his arm. Help me up?

She looks at it.

He stretches out his hand. She takes it, and he gives her his weight so she has to roll back on her heels to keep from falling as he stands. Please don't let her mother be looking. If Abe were closer, she'd tell him to get inside the thrift store, quick, like in her nightmares of a lone lion walking down the sunlit village street.

It'd be nice if she could send her thoughts into her brother's mind, and then he'd just do what she wanted. Some people think she and him can do that since they're twins. Got that twin magic, don't you?

Frank groans and coughs as he stands. Then he hangs his arm over Heza's shoulders. He's shorter than she is, and the height difference and his weight force her into a crouch.

You're heavy, she says.

Probably don't smell too good either, he says.

It's true. He smells like cigars and sweat. Smelling another person always startles her.

Abe hurries forward to help.

Go help Mom, she says.

Why? he says, confused.

Never mind, she says. She can't think of why. Later, she will think of these words again and again. *Go help Mom.* These will be haunting words. But right now the words are confused and in the way. *Go help Mom.* Why? I don't know.

I'll take the help, says Frank and raises his other arm for draping over Abe's shoulders.

Oh, wait, Abe says and goes back for the crutch. He offers it to Frank, but of course the crutch is taller than Frank too.

Damn, Abe says.

Frank loops his arm over Abe. Heza and Abe bend in a crouch and shuffle backwards with Frank, who seems to have trouble catching the ground with his feet.

The crowd's quiet, watching and pushing softly to see better.

Who gave that kid a gun?

Wouldn't a real gun be louder?

Frank fell, didn't he?

He's no more dead than he's a terrorist. It's the circus, for Christ's sake. Lighten up.

But still.

If it were an act, wouldn't it be over by now?

Just watch.

Should someone call 9-1-1?

Maybe he had a heart attack or something, just coincidence about the kid and his toy gun.

Was it a toy?

When I was that age, I had a real gun.

Heza and Abe lower Frank to the curb. He holds his chest, coughs.

The kids back up.

Frank looks over his glasses. Everyone can see. He counts to ten.

Then he springs up, throwing out his arms.

The children stare.

Ta-da! he shouts. He claps his hands.

Clap, he whispers to Heza and Abe.

They look at each other. They start clapping.

Jump up and down, Frank whispers.

Heza and Abe jump up and down. They forget to keep clapping, then start again. Now the other children start clapping. Slowly at first. Then faster.

He's alive! Heza shouts.

More applause.

Frank winks at her.

Amen! Abe shouts.

No, Heza says, but Abe ignores her.

He lives! Abe shouts.

Circus isn't a revival, Heza says.

It's resurrection, ain't it? says Abe.

Frank removes an invisible hat from his head and raises it high. Then he bows, sweeping low.

The kids hoot.

The adults laugh.

Some kids whistle, or try to. Hard to whistle while smiling.

Frank saunters back to the camper and climbs up the ladder. He stands up on the roof.

The boss hits the music. The speakers blare. The people jump.

Frank cartwheels to the front of the van, then leaps backward into a handspring, returning to where he started. He extends his arms and thanks the slick surface of the camper for not breaking him against the ground, here at the last village of the circuit, end of the season, three days before retirement.

Hezada! Frank shouts.

Hezada! the people shout back and applaud, rain catching between their palms.

41

The tumblers run up the street and jump high into the splits. When they land, they raise their arms to the applause, then take off again, running, jumping, now twisting too many times to count before they land facing the other side of the street. More applause. They rise up on their toes, arch their backs, and reach as though to touch the sky, defiant at the rain.

Would you look at that.

Never can believe it.

They cartwheel. They grab each other's hands. They climb onto each other's shoulders. They form a pyramid. Another claps his hands, trying to get the villagers to clap too, and a few do. Then he climbs to the top of the highest tumbler's shoulders.

Think it'll rain the whole time?

Hope not.

Supposed to.

Elephant come by yet?

It just started.

Guess not, then.

Elephants are always at the end.

Do they even have elephants anymore? Heard there won't be elephants at the circus here pretty soon. Because of the abuse.

Abuse-a-smoosh. That's all made up. My cousin worked a whole summer at the circus, not this one, but one like it, and he said he never saw anybody lay a hand on any elephant.

I read an article about it.

Don't mean it's true.

Why would anyone make that up?

People are crazy for attention these days, that's why. Or they're liberals.

That too.

Anyhow, there were only two elephants last year. Seems like I read they were down to one.

You see that lion down at the new pizza place in town?

Joe's?

Not Joe's anymore. But yeah, where Joe's used to be. Same building, across from Stoutin's. Pizza, yes. Just not Joe's Pizza.

You don't say?

I do.

This time, they chuckle.

Is it good?

Oh, you know. Pizza's pizza, not cut into squares like Joe's did, which I thought was weird myself, but this lion, you should go just to see it. Kid who owns the place, his grandfather or great-grandfather shot it. Circus lion. Escaped, I guess, off the train years and years ago.

That right?

Said so on the menu.

Never heard of that. Which train, anyway?

Used to be a train that ran from here to the town.

Can you touch it?

It's in a glass display case. You can touch the case, I guess.

Heck of a thing, shooting a lion.

Now come the jugglers. One throws a bowling pin into the air, rain spinning off it. The other juggler catches it. The people clap. A waitress whistles against her fingers.

The people turn to look at her.

She shrugs. It embarrasses my kids too, she says.

They laugh.

Tightrope always was my favorite.

Trapeze.

Which day you going?

Oh, this is probably enough for me.

You should go.

Gone nearly sixty summers. By now, there's not a place in the world they haven't shown me in those tents of theirs.

Hey, I'll buy your ticket.

No thanks.

If you change your mind…

If I do, my wife will tell you.

More laughter.

A small car swerves up the street. A pile of clowns wave. They lean their white faces and painted smiles out the windows. One honks the horn. Another honks his nose. Kiddies always like that, no matter the day or age.

Beepity-beep-beep.

Here come the horses clomping forward, their horseshoes ringing off the street and ricocheting off the buildings. Women stand on the horses' backs, waving.

There's the semi-truck pulling the flatbed that's tied down with tent poles and thick rolls of canvas. The driver waves too, though he hardly lifts his hand off the door. Never has known whether to wave or not.

But if the applause comes, then why not?

42

Heza and Abe's mother stands inside the thrift store watching the circus roll past.

They're my age now, Kae thinks about the women standing on the horses that clomp past the thrift store window. She feels herself not waving. Feels her hands tighten on her arms.

The parade used to be her favorite part, besides the shake-up stand.

There's her daughter, Heza, coming up the street. At least she and Jude gave up on leading the whole shebang. Though it's interesting that they thought to, that they'd clearly planned it without her knowing. But that's kids, isn't it?

And there's Abe on his skateboard with that crutch. Hopefully, he brings it back before he forgets it somewhere. It belongs in the basket with the other canes, crutches, and umbrellas.

Careful, kiddo, she thinks as he rows by. He seems to be racing the lions.

The bells clank against the door.

Morning, Kae says to the old woman.

The old woman says it's always a good morning when the circus comes.

That's what they say, Kae says. Kae shifts away from the window, like a plant tired of the sun.

The old woman is friends with Kae's mother. Or used to be. Her mother hasn't said much about her lately. But that's how friends work around here, in cycles. Visit every day for a year, then don't even say hello at the grocery.

Of course, circus isn't for everyone, says the old woman. She watches Kae's face.

Kae holds still so she won't seem sad, stricken, hurt, pained, distressed.

It's a hard time for you, says the old woman.

It's a hard time for lots of people, Kae says.

But not like it is for you.

It's a beautiful time too.

The woman winks.

Past is past, Kae says. She shrugs. If she weren't living this life, she would have overlooked it the same as she overlooks the trillions of strangers breathing right now, whose lives could have been hers.

One day she was waiting outside the diner to start her shift, next she's in line for a lemon shake-up, then in the church basement at her own baby shower, and now she's older than the acrobats and her kids are younger than that.

The old woman lowers her voice. If you want your cards read, she says, you come by any time.

Didn't know you still did that.

I don't make it a secret, but I don't broadcast it either. You know people.

I guess, Kae says.

No charge, of course.

I'll keep it in mind.

I told you about them babies, didn't I?

Kae forces a smile. She had sat at the woman's cluttered coffee table, listening to the thwick of the cards as the woman laid out her future, or someone's. But what village girl ever knocked on the fortuneteller's door after the circus and didn't turn out pregnant?

You be careful, says the old woman.

I wonder, Kae thinks, whether the old woman waits for her words to make meaning, or if the meaning just intensifies with time.

She has to lean against the window to see the caravan now. She can feel the window move with her weight.

43

The last of the caravan is now entirely off Main Street and winding through the park. The road is dark with rain. The few children in the playground leap off slides and out of swings, free in the air for one perfect moment before hitting the ground and stumbling forward.

44

There it goes, folks, says Abe.

They watch after the caravan.

They watch the people outside the diner watching after the caravan.

Jude sees her mother in the window, her forehead against the glass, watching the circus disappear. That lonely, wistful look on her mother's face awakens an urge in Jude to punish her.

She turns away from Heza and Abe, then back. She's got the tennis balls stuck up her shirt again. She says, Perhaps one of you circus people will do me the honor, and marry me out of this place.

Not again, Heza says. Your mom's nice.

I'll marry you, Abe says, then blushes.

Jude sashays toward Heza.

Cut it out, Heza says.

Jude purses her lips.

Kiss me, Hezada, Jude says, and rolls one hip back, then forward.

I'm serious, Jude.

And I'm so lonely, Jude says in her mother-mocking voice. But she feels sick, remembering her mother say nearly the same words.

I'm lonely, Jude, said her mother as they laid on the couch watching TV, another romance about a country woman whose life is redeemed by finding a man one step stronger than she is, to do her right by elevating her out of single-mother status, or young-widow status, or spinster-rancher status, to wife.

I hope you're never lonely like this, Jude's mother said to her.

Heza sees Jude's face change, her lips gone serious.

Jude?

Hezada, Jude says.

Heza steps back.

Jude reaches for Heza's face.

Heza ducks and turns.

People can't see.

Jude takes a step forward, forgetting to keep her back arched, and the tennis balls fall out of her shirt. One bounces across the sidewalk and the other goes into the street. The rain increases in intensity, as though on cue.

Ah, hell, Jude says because a car's coming. A slow, old maroon car. The lady peering over the steering wheel won't see the ball and clearly missed the arrival of the circus.

There's relief in being able to look away. Heza says, Wait for it.

Wait for it, Jude says.

Wait for it.

They laugh.

But the ball rolls right under the car, missing all the tires, somehow, and to the curb where it starts following the gutter down the street. The old woman honks, even though the girls run behind her. The girls laugh and wave at the rear windshield. They dance around, feeling silly and brave. They duck under the thrift-store awning, which is striped because it used to be a barber shop.

Jude stops the ball with the side of her foot and picks it up. She looks at Heza. You sick or something?

Heza laughs and runs back to Jude's doorway. Is she sick? Did her mother see? She turns to see Jude running after her.

Abe says, We going to the pool, or what?

Not if lightning comes, says Jude.

Besides, Heza says, thought you wanted to earn free tickets for helping the circus set up.

I can do both, he says.

He's full of dreams, Heza says to Jude.

Nothing wrong with that, Jude says.

Abe grins at Jude.

Maybe Mom will buy us lunch at the circus, Abe says.

Won't be set up in time.

Tomorrow, maybe, Abe says.

If tomorrow is always tomorrow, sure.

She don't like the circus much, does she? Jude says.

She likes it alright, Abe says.

Except she doesn't, Heza says.

Because of your dad, right? Jude says.

Yeah.

You think he's dead?

Don't talk like that, says Jude's mother, now dressed for work and coming down the stairs.

It's okay, says Heza. We never met him.

I know it, you poor thing, Jude's mother says and presses Heza's face against her chest. She smells like detergent and cigarette smoke. Jude rolls her eyes. Heza grins at her. Thank God you still got your mother. Do you thank God for that?

I do, says Heza.

Good girl. Jude, you should thank God for your mother like Heza does.

Thought you weren't on the schedule, Jude says and points at the pens in her mother's apron pocket.

First day of the circus. They'll need help and tips are better.

You said we could go get my school supplies.

You acted like that wasn't something you wanted to do.

Jude shrugs.

You know how she *loves* school, Ada says to Heza.

I like the pencils and stuff, anyway, says Jude.

We'll go tomorrow.

Tomorrow's the weekend.

Your dad can take you, then.

But y—

Circus is in town, Jude. We need the money. She hates saying it, but it's true. Landlord still hasn't reimbursed her for the extra cost on last month's utility bill after the water pipe burst by the toilet, and now the circus, which is fun if you've got spending money, and depressing as hell if you don't. Plus school supplies. Money, money, money. Don't think about it too hard or it's already spent. Probably Jude's grown out of last year's winter coat. Did she even get a new winter coat last year?

Then Ada's hurrying up the sidewalk toward the diner, holding her apron over her head for an umbrella.

45

It's still raining, and the next truck to roll up the village street is a work truck. A bunch of teenagers sit in the bed, dirty from detasseling all morning in the fields. The rain drips off the bills of their hats, trickles mud into their ears and down their necks. A few stretch their shirts over their heads for makeshift umbrellas. Others press their faces to the sky, letting the rain flicker off their eyelashes. Like when we were little.

Good times.

Those were the days.

But this rain feels good after all morning.

Got one! a girl says, after closing her mouth on a raindrop.

You think it's easier working in the rain?

No way, says one.

Hell if it ain't, says another.

Makes me start wishing I was at the pool.

You too?

Which makes it worse because you have to keep stopping yourself from thinking about the pool. Maybe that's just me.

What I do is I imagine a little pond waiting for me at the end of each row, and I think, when I get there, I'll dive right in.

That'd drive me crazy.

Didn't say I wasn't crazy. Just saying how I get to the end of the row.

How do you start the next row?

Move the pond.

They laugh. But the kid's serious about moving the pond and serious about feeling crazy, the way the heat locks around his head all day, the way the sun just won't stop. The way there's always another row. Last night when he got home, he clutched the sides of his bedroom mirror and stared into it, so close his nose touched his nose.

Who are you? he said.

Who are you? his mirror said. Or he said. Or they're the same. Can they be?

Half the kids who start detasseling at the beginning of summer quit by day two. These kids in the truck are the ones who made it, if enduring torture for money is making it.

There's pride in it, anyway, the staying, since they don't have lives that allow for quitting on day two. They will feel similarly in a few years when they go to the recruiter's office in the shopping mall and join the military. The ones who make it through will be flown from base to base, war to war, until tattoos cross their hearts, hook their sides, spread across their backs, and vine their arms.

Arms that, right now, feel hollow after working all morning, not to mention scratched to hell even with the sleeves rolled down and the cuffs buttoned. The kid always telling stories says, Last year, or the year before, there was a kid that wore short sleeves every day. Every. Day.

No way, someone says.

Absolutely, he says.

You knew the kid?

Of course I did.

Wasn't no kid like that.

Sure there was.

And he lasted the whole summer?

He did, but they had to remove his left arm because it got way infected. We kept telling him, Man, something's wrong with your arm, but he didn't believe it. But then it started smelling. And we told him, can't you smell that stink? And maybe he could, but maybe his pride didn't let him smell it, or admit to smelling it. We all noticed, and said, Man, a doctor needs to look at that, but he'd never been to a doctor in his life, and he'd just shrug and say he was fine. At least wash them good when you get home, we'd say. But he didn't.

Let me guess. A Henderson.

You'd think so, but this was some kid visiting some relative or another.

Who visits for a summer and gets a job detasseling? That's how I know there wasn't any such kid.

A migrant is who.

Listen, at the end of the day, this kid's arm, the wound, looked like he'd been buried alive and dug up a few years later.

He work next season?

No.

Because he had only one arm?

Naw. He kilt himself.

What kind of fucking story is that?

Jesus.

That's how it happened. You want me to say that didn't happen? Fine. Kid went back home, got himself a robot arm, became an Olympian, and made a world record throwing the discus. He lives somewhere in Tel Aviv or something, with a model for a wife and all his kids have one arm, just like him. And if you don't believe me, you can go visit a statue of him up at the county courthouse. That the kind of ending you like?

The truck pulls up to the curb. The kids climb over the side or jump the tailgate. Pieces of field fall out of their pants. One picks a tick from his neck and says goddamn. He pinches the tick between his fingers and takes a lighter from his pocket. The girls lean away.

Flick it or something.

Only way to kill a tick is fire or toilet.

The kid holding the tick smiles. He reaches into the truck bed for an empty pop bottle. He drops the tick inside and takes a receipt from his pocket and scrunches it into the bottle until just a corner's sticking out. He flicks the lighter and sets the corner on fire. He pushes it the rest of the way in, then holds the bottle up so everyone can see the paper burning inside it.

Die, motherfucker, the boy says and shakes the bottle. The fire climbs down the receipt. Starts treading the last sip of coke.

The others look at his face. Some chuckle, others grimace.

That'll learn you, the boy says.

Won't learn anything if it's dead, a girl says.

It's a tick.

I'm just saying.

He glares at her.

She glares back.

He screws the lid back on, watching her as he does it. She knows he's threatening her, but she doesn't look away. Her mother taught her that. She watches until the fire goes out, and the smoke presses its tentacles against the plastic. The boy looks at the bottom of the bottle until he finds the tick.

You can't hide, he says and flips the bottle over and over.

Like a goddamned carnival ride, he says, laughing. What's it called? The Zipper? The Kamikaze? He flips it again. Yeah, The Kamikaze. He wishes someone would give him that nickname. It'd be cool to be called Kamikaze.

They leave him standing there and head to the diner. People leave as they go in.

Wish it'd stop raining, one of the boys says.

Don't be a pussy, says another boy.

Hey! says a girl, like she's offended but not offended. Like she's supposed to be put-off but isn't. The boys smirk and glance at the other girls. The girls smile because they don't know what else to do.

I mean for the party tonight. Shitty if it got rained out.

What party?

You're not invited.

Everybody's invited. Even him.

Ha. Ha.

Look at this, says one of the kids, reaching down and picking up a red-foiled candy.

Look, there's another one.

Now they're looking down at the sidewalk and along the gutters.

You hear that?

What?

That. Music. *That.*

She does.

And he does.

He does too.

One by one, they hear it and nod at each other as they recognize it, and the more they see each other recognize the same music, they smile, wider and wider.

You know what that means?

Maybe a longer lunch.

That and it's gonna be the best circus party ever.

Fuck yeah.

We should make it go down in history.

They think of the stories of the best circus parties. Tales of cars and trucks parked for miles of country road just to get into the party out in the forest. Police cars too, because everybody's invited. Everybody. So big you could see the bonfire from space and without a parent knowing about it.

Absolutely we should.

We'll invite the circus. Acrobats, clowns, the whole shebang.

They laugh.

But the kid with a smile means it, you can tell by his face.

Seriously!

You really are crazy.

Think about it, though.

They do. Clowns tapping plastic beer cups with them. The trapeze artist doing a keg stand. Lions trotting in circles around the bonfire. The glitter of sequins. The tattooed woman telling stories off her skin.

Awesome.

You think they'd come?

We're the last stop, aren't we?

They clap hands. They hug. They imagine walking the power lines above the country roads, their shadows like clouds over the cornfields. It's so much better than the cold shower and clean clothes they usually imagine to make it through the day, and both are pretty damn good.

Maybe we should invite our parents.

What?

My mom would dig it.

The kids laugh. What a good fool that kid is.

As they inch along the wall, waiting for a table to open up, they're sneaking into the night of their imaginations, climbing into each other's cars, heading out to the kid's grandfather's land, where they will have the best party of their ever-loving lives, if not the best circus party in the history of the village and the ever-loving world.

46

In the diner, the waitresses move with a bright lightness around tables. Taking plates. Refilling coffees. Leaving another straw, another pitcher of syrup, another check.

Most are mothers, a few grandmothers, and there's only two times a year when customers tip what they always should: Christmas and the day the circus rolls in. As soon as the circus music reaches their ears, customers reach for the waitresses.

Come here a second, they say, and slip a fiver, maybe a twenty, into their hands, their aprons, into the back pocket of their jeans.

Instead of saying, You sure look nice today—

Instead of saying, That a new perfume?

That necklace sure does look nice on you—

Today, they drop the tip and say, You tell Randy, You tell your Amy, You tell your little ones to absolutely spend all of this in one place.

Sure is nice of you.

Well, it's the circus.

Oh, you don't have to go and do that.

Sure, it's the circus.

The circus.

The circus is here. Everybody deserves a little fun. Only young once.

Only young again at the circus.

Circus is in town.

And, it's true, the circus may be here now, but the waitresses know they'll have to pay back the customers the rest of the year. They will laugh at their dirty jokes. They'll find phone numbers under coffee mugs left by other women's husbands. They'll see the winks. They'll scrub off dick graffiti in the bathrooms. They'll walk by booths filled with oilfield men and feel their eyes and thoughts roll down their arms, under their breasts, inside their thighs.

Yes, there will be payment for today's generosity. A kind of tired savings account that only baby Jesus and acrobats can unlock, and only the waitresses must pay back.

But they can't think about it that way today, because health insurance don't pay for itself, and tips is tips, even when the circus is in town.

You gonna take the kids? calls out the waitress refilling coffee from across the room to the waitress counting salad plates.

Hell no, she says. I'm going by myself!

The cooks laugh, the waitresses laugh, the customers laugh. A few ask, What'd she say?

Said she was going by herself.

That right? The few laugh.

It can't be wrong, the waitress hollers.

Now, I heard that!

The laughter grows. The food tastes better. The ceiling fans reflect more clearly in the coffee. The line cook ladles the gravy into the mashed potatoes with a flourish. The other cook grins that grimace of his. Here's the dishwasher, emerging from the back, carrying a gray bus tub, to clear the tables himself. Look there, even the owner hefts himself out of the back booth and makes his way to the cash register. Doesn't matter that he wears those tight diabetes socks. Doesn't matter that he has to squint even with his reading glasses. Doesn't matter that he can't remember the newest prices or what the regulars order. He smiles. He takes the bills. He offers up the basket of miniature peanut butter cups and tears off the 10-cent price tag, stuffing it into his breast pocket. Thank you for coming. Good to see you again. Glad you're still kicking.

Not like I used to.

Can't do the cancan forever.

Isn't that the truth?

You have a good day now.

You too.

You too.

Like when he opened the diner forty years ago. What plans he had.

Come again, you hear?

Always do, Bill.

Sure, Bill, sure.

Good to see you.

The diner door jangles. Another table leaves, another table enters, and someone holds the door. More customers today, and more customers ordering food, not just coffee or a milkshake. Next three days will be like this too, busier, faster—a pulsing as strangers drive in, parking on both sides of the street because it's free to walk to the circus instead of paying to park in the farmer's field across from it.

Good to see you.

Good to see *you*.

Yes.

It is.

47

She's having that faraway feeling. It always passes. But it always comes back too. She never knows what to do with it. It's uncomfortable, like before throwing up. This feeling that she's not quite right. Not sick. But not right in some inside way. Usually when she feels like this, she'll go change her clothes, even though it doesn't change the feeling. She remembers asking her mother about it, but her mother just checked her for a fever.

Not warm, her mother said.

I know. It's not that. It's...

What? her mother said.

Just feel weird.

You're not weird.

Sort of.

Not bad weird, though. Everybody feels weird around here.

Except that they don't.

Maybe they don't say it out loud, her mother said, but that doesn't mean they don't feel that way. I felt weird growing up.

Now you don't?

I don't think I'd go as far as to say that.

Maybe she just needs to be alone. She could go out to the creek. It's quiet out there.

48

You coming or not? Abe says. Mom said we have to stick together.

We could go to the swimming pool, Heza says.

Remember about my mother, Jude says and holds the tennis balls to her chest.

Oh yeah.

We could go look for the buried elephant, Heza says. Abe says he knows where it might be.

Do you? Jude says.

Abe shrugs. Maybe.

You do not, Jude says.

Nobody's going to find it during the circus. Can't dig in the field the circus is right on top of.

Jude looks at Heza. You sick or something?

I don't know, Heza says. No. She examines Jude's face. The smooth curves that slope from her nose into her cheeks. The freckles speckling her forehead and chin.

That's pretty, Heza says.

Pretty gray, Jude says, looking at the sky.

Gray can be nice.

Jude shrugs. So you wanna go look for the elephant? Rain might raise the bones enough to see them. Happened to my uncle. When his dog died, he didn't bury it deep enough, and one time it rained all day, maybe a couple days, until the dog came back out of the ground.

That's awful, says Heza.

Yeah.

What happened then?

He had to bury it again, says Jude.

You think it's real or made up?

Why would my uncle lie about that?

I mean about the elephant, Heza says.

Never thought about it, Jude says. Which part?

All the parts, maybe. Maybe the dying part most of all. Never heard about an elephant killing itself.

Except that you have, because we know about this elephant.

But outside of this one.

How many suicided elephants you got to hear about to believe it?

Dunno, Heza says. Three, five, maybe?

More than one.

More than one, definitely.

Jude laughs and starts walking toward the park. Heza stands a while more before following Jude up the street. If the rain stopped that very moment and a rainbow or three beamed across the sky, she wouldn't have noticed. Because of love, that hope.

49

Out of the park, between gray sky and gray road, the children follow the circus caravan on their bikes like a colorful kite tail made of rain slickers. Their bike tires hiss against the wet road. They lean forward. They keep their heads down. They pedal hard. Some try to jump their bikes over the ditch into the field. Some go sliding. Some fall sideways, smearing into the mud, up their legs and arms. Others complete the jump, cross to the other side, and laugh in surprise as they glance back at the muddy ruts following them.

But it's so muddy all the kids who ride into the field have to dismount a few feet in. They start walking. The wet field is heavy against their shoes. A few lose their shoes and have to hop back, the toes of their socks dangling. Several stoop and tie their shoes tighter, or roll up their pants and take off their socks and shoes. Some see it all and stay on the road, gliding along or brake-pedal-braking to keep just enough momentum while keeping near the kids in the field.

Think they'll cancel?

The circus?

No way.

What if it doesn't stop?

The rain?

Yeah.

Like ever?

Yeah.

Like forever-ever?

Yeah.

Well, I guess we'll all drown, so probably the circus would just stay here.

I don't want to die.

Me neither.

It's not going to rain that long, is it?

Naw. But you'll still die.

Yeah.

Up ahead, two circus workers walk an invisible line in opposite directions. The men carry the orange spray-painted metal stakes that will run the perimeter of the field and hold up the orange plastic fence. They stop. They lift mallets and drive in a stake. Then walk again.

Over there looks to be the man from last year. He's wearing a see-through poncho and driving a four-wheeler with someone on the back who's unrolling the orange fence as they surge forward.

Maybe he'll ask them again this year for help raising the tents or building the metal fence around the Ferris wheel. If there is a Ferris wheel this year. Or maybe that's the fair. No, seems like it's the circus too. Or walking the tigers.

What?

Maybe.

Never know.

I think I know whether you can walk the tigers.

You think you know everything.

Go ask him.

You go ask him.

Maybe if he sees us, he'll ask.

The kids wait. The man in the poncho revs the handle of the

four-wheeler. The woman behind him unravels more fence and hooks it onto the metal stakes.

I could climb over that.

Anybody could.

Then why have a fence at all?

So you know not to.

Go ask him already.

About the tigers?

About working for tickets.

The main path that serves as the circus's midway is made from summer after summer of people walking away the grass so by now it's lower than the rest of the field. And now it's filled with rain, more trench than path.

On both sides of the trench-path trudges a group of people in dollar-bin ponchos or trash bags slit open for their heads. On their feet are rain boots or hiking boots. One woman wears a plastic bag on her head, handles knotted at her chin like a bonnet.

The other half of the group doesn't have rain protection and shuffles along in bare arms and T-shirts that cling to their backs. Now and then, one hitches up jeans gone heavy with rain and mud. It'll take days for their tennis shoes to dry, and even longer before the smell fades.

Just ahead of this group of workers rolls a truck with its tailgate down. When it stops, they reach in and pull bags of tents out, slinging them into the field as they do. The truck starts again. They follow. It stops. They pull more bags of canvas and metal poles onto the ground.

It's slow work, which makes it harder work, and it's work that doesn't allow for thoughts so at the end of the day, when thoughts come, the people don't know what to do with them and sit, stunned.

Or the thoughts weight their bodies into sleep and nightmares they hopefully won't remember by morning.

Most of this group has worked this job for so many years that the summers have compressed their spines in wrong ways, thrown pelvises, pinched nerves in their shoulders that explode or numb at the slightest movement.

They lean.

They reach.

They swing each bundle onto one side of the path or the other.

They lean.

They reach.

Could add up all the miles they've walked individual-wise or group-wise, and they could have walked to Alaska and back, probably more than once. Maybe all the way up to the melting ice caps. But there's no time for thinking that. That's for later, when their thoughts punish them for not paying attention.

Or Mexico. Probably about the same distance. Hard to know.

Plenty of workers you could ask.

Once they reach the end of the midway, the truck will brake, and they'll pull their bodies into the truck bed, and the truck will carry them back to the start.

Here, it's happening.

The kids wait and listen to the rain drumming against the plastic covering the people's backs. They reach for each other's hands. A woman slips, then rights herself. Could have been bad.

The truck's brake lights go dark, and the driver throws his arm over the cab seats and looks over his shoulder as he reverses up the midway.

Now the group gets off, two by two, to set up each tent. By the time they reach the middle, they join together to raise up the largest tent, the Big Top.

It's a giant tent, larger than most houses around here, and older than most people around here, if not older than their good, dead mothers. Fabric's newer, but the frame's older. All around the perimeter, the workers stand, holding poles, pulling ropes, throwing a rope to the nearest person. But before the canvas goes up, it's just the frame, the tent's skeleton unfolding.

Wet enough for ya?

Not yet.

For me it is.

Least it makes the ground give.

Sure, but rain keeps up, ground'll give too much, and one wind from the right direction could take down every tent.

A man snaps his fingers.

Another man watches, imagining it. Just like that.

Didn't see it was supposed to rain like this.

Weather around here.

That's for sure.

Not just here. Weather's changing everywhere.

Three, four hurricanes on the same day. Worst hurricanes ever recorded. Since records started being kept, anyway.

What's your point? Haven't been recording for that long.

Least a hundred years.

Not that long in the scheme of things, really.

Scientists say it's no good.

Oh, okay. You're one of those.

One of those?

Think you know enough to know what scientists are talking about. Scientists don't know shit.

That right?

That's right. They're paid by the government. You know that, right? That they're paid by the United States government?

What branch?

Whaddya mean?

What branch of government pays them, pays these scientists, if you know so goddamn much about it?

Don't have to know.

That right?

That's right. Weather's weather. Weather's the way it always has been.

Except that it isn't. Just the other day, an article in the paper talked about how the whole world's heating up. Hotter than ever. New records every month.

Don't feel hotter to me.

Hell, they was even talking about it on the radio when we were driving here. You heard it, same as I did.

I know what I heard.

What'd you hear if it wasn't that?

A bunch of bullcrap is what I heard. A bunch of conspiracy theories except all you people that think you're so fancy smart never think your beliefs are conspiracy theories.

Fancy smart?

That's right. Next thing you're gonna tell me you believe in scientists, but you don't believe in God. I know the way you people think.

You people? What's that mean?

You know.

Oh yeah?

Yeah.

Everyone watches the two men. If those were fighting words or not. Usually there's two, three fights a week, always at setup or tear-down. Because work like this does something to you. The heat of it. What it does to the body. How it erases all your thoughts so that you don't remember how to think for a while, sometimes ever, if you want the truth about it. All of them feel it. When there's a next stop, the two men switch sides, and argue it the other way, just because they need to argue. Need to feel some kind of conviction about this world that moves them more than they move it.

Around here, beliefs don't mean much.

50

A man in a yellow raincoat stands in the entryway of the circus field. This is where the circus-goers will enter and exit under the archway a blacksmith made years ago. From the archway will hang the circus sign, which is lit by old bulb lights so thin and clear you can see the filaments.

A truck is backing up the road with two ticket booths strapped to its flatbed. The man in the yellow raincoat gestures, and the truck's tires begin turning.

The man signals.

The truck stops. It pulls forward. The tires straighten out.

The man moves his hands. The tires turn. An elbow appears out the window. Rain's hammering off the side mirror. Through the mirror he can see the driver's oil-stained hands on the steering wheel, the set of his mouth.

Come on, he mutters at the person directing him in.

This shouldn't be difficult, mutters the man in the raincoat.

The back tires lower into the field. The ticket booths strain against the belts holding them around their waists.

There we go. Now the truck's got it. Maybe.

He starts walking backward now, motioning to the side mirror to keep coming. Just like that. Just like. Good.

It's no picnic, but it's better than smashing the skulls of baby pigs at the meat-processing plant. Which is what he used to do with fifty other men in a long metal building off a country road like this one right here. Sometimes when the tires on the truck are at a certain angle, trying to do a tight turn, there's this awful metal-to-metal squeal that sends his brain right back to the plant, to the scream of the pigs—the sound of rubber boots against the cement floor—the slap and slush of the squeegee he used to push the pigs' blood off the floor. So much blood it puddled and rippled against the squeegee he pushed—bright red waves along the cement floor.

It's no picnic, that's for damn sure, he'd heard more than one man say.

Say that again.

That's for sure.

And it never leaves you, he'd say if he was on break too, smoking cigarettes in the field behind the awful building. All the meat-men smoked because none could stomach eating on a break, and smoking took their appetites so they didn't have to think about hunger.

It never leaves you, he whispers to the kids watching the circus set up from their bikes, even though they can't hear. He hopes they don't wind up in the same place or someplace like it, though more than a few will, whether they hear him or not.

Of course, this job's a little more dangerous. For him, anyway. Last summer, he was backing a ticket booth off the truck, and the booth started tipping, and the belt holding it snapped, and it started sliding down off the trailer toward him. He felt electric, and his head filled with the high-pitched screams of the pigs and the anxious laughter of the men who killed them.

Jump! someone yelled.

He jumped, and as his body took to the air, he remembered the pigs watching other pigs being killed. Their big brown eyes, their long eyelashes coarse against the palm of his hand when he covered their eyes before slitting their throats.

I have eyes, he thought as he jumped.

Who's watching my eyes? he thought as he jumped.

Surely he wasn't suspended in the air that long, but in his memory, he's there forever, just as, in another memory, his only child is suspended forever sideways in the blue-gloved hands of the surgeon who lifted her from the slit belly of his girlfriend and into the bright hospital lights, her small mouth open in confusion and wail.

When he heard the anxious laughter from his own mouth, he quit the meat-processing plant.

Get the fuck out, he said on his drive home from work that day, after he'd picked up his daughter from day care. He glanced into the rear-view mirror. She watched him from her car seat.

You shouldn't say that, she said.

I know, baby. Sorry.

Okay, she said.

Get the fuck out, he said.

Dad.

I know. Sorry. He turned off the radio and rolled up the windows so it was fully quiet as they drove home. The smell of him and his work marinating. He didn't like picking her up after his work because of that, or driving her in this car, which was bled through with the smell of dead pigs and his life. But her mother had to cover a shift, and so.

For most of the decade he worked at the plant, the other men called him a lucky son-of-a because he wasn't in love, married, or a father, though he'd come close to all of those. And then his daughter happened. So the newest kid at the plant became the lucky son-of-a.

But he'd heard that laugh, and the laugh was from his own mouth. Get the fuck out, he whispered.

Daddy, she said.

Sorry. Don't tell your mother.

We're not supposed to say that.

You're right, you're right. You can tell your mother. No lies.

No lies.

That's right.

That night, he called up the manager and said he quit.

At least give me your two weeks.

I've given you ten years, he thought but didn't say.

Fine.

But two days later, he left at smoke break, and that was that. His daughter's mother was angry, of course. Because bills. Because how will they ever get ahead now? Because you don't get to up and quit. You're the man. You're a father now. Why don't you seem to understand that? What part of you can't get that?

He thought of his baby daughter suspended in the lights, held aloft by those blue gloves.

I'll find another job.

Nobody finds another job around here. Not when you quit like that.

Surely they do.

But she'd been more right than she'd really ever been, and he entered into a kind of shunning by the town. First, he thought it was just the men he used to work with who were ignoring him. But soon he noticed it was everyone in the diner when he and she and their daughter came in for breakfast. He could tell they were doing it on purpose, because if they'd been strangers, everyone would have stared. No one even looked.

He'd broken an unspoken rule of the town, which was that everyone has a lot in life, and not a good one. Jobs around here aren't good or easy, but you don't quit. Not like that, anyway.

He didn't blame them. But he couldn't say so or it'd sound like pitying them, and that could get him killed. Seems dramatic, maybe. But to survive the life that insists on being his, he has to think like that.

It's pretty easy to stay away from the circus animals, though he hadn't believed it when the circus boss had said so in the interview.

But it is.

The animals stay toward the back. He stays at the front. They shuffle through the back of the big tent. He walks out the front. None are pigs, which helps, but he worries that the animals will still sense it on him—what he used to do. He doesn't want them to know.

But this job is better than the one before. And he only works summers and sends all the money, except eating money, back to his daughter's mother. They didn't take to Florida at first. You don't know what the summers are like here, she'd say into the phone. There's a reason circus leaves during summers. Jesus, the tourists, she'd say.

But it made him laugh a little to have such a problem. The last paycheck of the season, he hand delivers to her.

51

One ticket booth goes here, the other by the rides and tents. He won't work the ticket booths, though, once he has them set up. That's what the retired women performers do, though he hears most die before retirement. From broken necks, or love, or both. They're supposed to use nets, but not all the performers do. Most don't. Because applause. Because the circus boss slips them an envelope. The more daring, the more money. A dead circus performer can grow a bigger audience than a living one.

Because it is what it is.

He works the giant slide, sometimes the carousel. He prefers the carousel, taking tickets, helping the littler ones onto the wooden rabbits, the unicorns, the stationary lion with its endless roar.

Use two hands, he reminds the kids, looking into big eyes to make sure they've heard.

Stand closer, he says to the parents who ride with their kids. Put your hand here, he says. Hold there.

Of course, some parents watch from the ground. Probably to keep from throwing up. Equilibrium seems to change as you age. Did for him, anyway, in his early thirties. So he doesn't blame them or think they're shitty parents for letting the kids ride alone. His daughter's mother has a thing about bridges—can't drive over them. Who's he to tell her she shouldn't fear bridges?

Some of these circus workers, though, and he knows who they are, they don't watch the kids close enough. He can tell immediately which carousel rider will fall apart on the ride, scream for Mama, try to scramble off the yawning tiger for the whirling ground where Mama stands without moving, somehow. Which is terrifying in itself.

For one, it's never the shy kid. It's almost always the loud talker, the one that won't shut up in line, going on and on about how great this is gonna be, how he's gonna ride that chicken—no the rabbit—no the chicken, right over the moon.

It was the same with the piglets.

He tries to tell the Summer Boys. Watch the talkers, he says.

What?

The talkers.

But the Summer Boys never understand, or none he's met. So he just swaps the slide for the carousel when he can. You can see the whole circus from up there, he tells them. That usually does it. Besides, it's true, you can. And they're young enough that such a sight won't break their hearts.

As he goes around the carousel, checking their safety belts and showing them how to hold the golden poles, he whispers fast to the loud kids. Little tips about what to do if their stomachs start to go. Or they start imagining the ride won't ever end.

You just bite your heels into the ribs of this here frog, this here horse, this here ostrich. He pushes their tennis shoes against the wooden creature so they can feel what he means.

You start feeling panicky, sweaty in your hands, you yell Help. Soon as I hear Help, I'll stop this ride, quick as you please, and none of the other kids will be the wiser.

He watches their eyes or until their heads nod so slightly.

Some workers won't stop the ride. Some let the ride go longer if a kid's crying. Like they're teaching the kid a good lesson that will harden him for his future.

Not him, though. No reason to let a kid cry. If you can help it, you should. And that's what he says at the end of the circus when he's drunk as a skunk, so drunk he's crying a little bit himself, trying to explain why you do what you can to help these little kids. And that's why the others like him. And why, since he started working here, each summer fewer people run the rides like it's only pulling a lever and saying exit through the back.

Of course, early or at the end of the season, most of the temporaries are gone, off to harvest fields for worse pay, but pay's pay, and anyone with a family should understand that. Every man or woman crawling through muddy fields picking blackberries has seen their child held up in the hospital lights.

So staff is short, but that's the only time he works one of the tents that get smaller toward the end of the midway, at the edge of lights where shadows creep into the dark. It's one performer per tent back there, one woman drumming behind the curtain before stepping naked onto a plywood stage and rolling her hips. Sometimes she wears the drum herself.

He doesn't like working those tents, except to keep the shitheads out. He doesn't like how much younger the girls look every summer, and how the men almost never are, even if that's the way it's always been.

There's something familiar to it that he don't like. Frank agrees, and said it best one night, when he found himself sitting under Frank's camper awning.

Thing of it is, Frank said, I never know whether I'm protecting them or killing them. Not killing them dead. Just parts of them that maybe they don't even know are dying.

The girls?

All of them. The whole goddamned thing.

Maybe it's not the truth, but it's closest he's come to it.

It's not what anyone imagines when he says he works for the circus, but he doesn't meet many new people to say it to anyway.

The nights are his favorite, when all the circus lights flicker over the midway from the tents, the criss-crossing strands, the glo-necklaces around the children's throats and wrists. The music's going and the circus-goers are strolling home, allowed to move slowly because their tickets are used and the show's over. He'll get this feeling in his chest, that something wonderful is happening despite the dark beyond the lights, and if he closes his eyes, it's only lights against his eyelids.

52

The thrift store door is locked when Jude and Heza try it.

Heza steps back, confused.

Jude crunches a lollipop between her teeth. Were you supposed to meet her for lunch?

Heza shakes her head slowly, but doesn't feel herself shaking her head or pressing her whole face against the glass door, nose smashed to one side. She cups her hands around her eyes, bringing the light of the store into view. The concrete floor. The racks of women's dresses like cloth bells of varying lengths. The counter is just inside the edge of her sight, but her mother isn't standing there.

Though Jude will never tell Heza, never think to tell her, she will always remember the dread, the smell of rain off hot asphalt, that pineapple-flavored lollipop.

The store shouldn't have been locked.

For a long time after this, Heza won't register having a body.

She begins to run.

53

The girls run through the village under the gray sky. The rain is lighter but steady.

The front yard of Heza's house is full of puddles, some spilling into other puddles. The car's in the driveway and should be, since her mother walks to work. I don't even know why we have a car. We wouldn't need one if the village still had a grocery.

Her mother has a yellow raincoat. Did she wear it this morning? Was it raining this morning when they walked with her to work? They walk with her every day, but today was the circus day. Abe had circled it a thousand times on the calendar. So they knew it was coming, the circus, and were talking about it. Worrying what would happen if it rained. Would it be cancelled? Was that even a thing? Their mother didn't remember it ever being cancelled. You'll have to ask your grandparents. They might remember. But probably not. This is how the circus people make their living, and rain's just a part of it.

It was strange to think of the circus people as working, as the circus being their job.

The front porch is empty except for the planter of purple petunias.

The front door's unlocked like always. Her mother doesn't open it and welcome the girls inside for lunch. She doesn't stand in the picture window, hanging up the yellow raincoat.

Her mother doesn't come down the stairs or around the corner. The laundry basket on the table is empty. Her mother's keys are on the table corner. Are those the keys to the thrift store or the car? Does she keep them on the same ring?

The kitchen is empty. Jude opens the refrigerator to see what's to eat. She likes that there's never any beer in this refrigerator.

Maybe she's at the diner like everybody else, Jude says to the grapes in the bottom drawer.

Heza pulls open the back door, its curtain wavering.

She walks into the backyard.

Past the clothesline.

Past her brother's bike.

Past the pile of plastic and terracotta planters her mother's always meaning to fill.

At the back of the yard is the old garage that's more a warning than a garage. Don't play in that. Roof could fall through at any moment. One day the landlord will pull it down, and maybe her mother believes him or maybe she just says so, but Heza and Abe never have. Its walls are gray and it smells like mildew and mice. They store the sleds and push mower in it, but I don't even like to, her mother says each summer before she rolls out the mower and each winter day she pulls down the sleds.

That's where Heza finds her mother.

54

I can't reach her.

The chair is on the floor sideways. It's the paint-spattered chair where Heza sat last October, a pumpkin wedged between her legs as she outlined a face to cut out.

This, Heza will think of later.

For now, she turns the chair upright.

She climbs onto it.

She cannot hear her own heart, loud as it is.

She can't hear herself screaming. Or how the garage traps it.

She can't hear Jude slamming out the back door of the house and running.

56

I can't reach you.

Help me, Heza's saying from the chair, her arms around her mother.

Help me.

How?

Jude's scanning the garage for a ladder, another chair to stack on this chair. But there's only a makeshift counter, a folded bag of potting soil. An orange plastic jack-o'-lantern on a shelf. A push mower. Pruning shears.

Heza's climbing down.

Get on my shoulders, Heza says.

Jude does.

Heza tries to climb onto the chair while holding Jude.

I can't do it! Heza cries.

Try these, Jude says.

Then the neighbor is coming up the alley, following the screams that found his quiet house on the other side of the fence.

58

Where's Abe? Someone needs to get Abe.

What do I tell him?

Just get him. Get him quick.

Abe's out in the circus field, crouched by a length of neon orange fencing. He's helping tie it to one of the stakes. He's wearing a rain hat that's not his; it's too big for him, and the rain drips off the bill and onto his bare arms.

His mother's dead. He doesn't know it.

60

Now comes the sound of sirens.

Now the circus boss turns, looking into the field. A child in a rain hat is running, dragging a crutch behind him.

The circus boss raises his camera to his eye. The gray sky, the muddy field. The child moves through the frame.

Then out, toward home and his mother.

As though Kae climbed into the sky, up, up, up as she held a wrinkled sheet wider than the world. Then she let go.

And now the sheet floats to the ground, covering the village, her children, everyone who is now left to kneel with small irons and the never-ending effort to smooth out all the wrinkles, the folds, the confusion of dirt that the world must be.

62

Later, many years later, Heza will walk with a friend who lost her brother the same way. And they will take turns trying to say what it's like. Heza will say, it's like our lives were a spiderweb, or my life was, and my mother threw a rock right through its center, and now my job is to try to match the threads back together.

But how can you?

As she says this, she will think of the spiderwebs that appeared on the bushes out front her childhood home, how the dew caught the light against the threads each morning. She'd take a stick to the webs, amazed every time at her ability to destroy—how easily the webs collapsed and clung to the weapon in her hand.

Abe comes home to vehicles in the driveway, along the front of the house, blocking the mailbox. There's people everywhere. A man stands by the door. Abe climbs the stairs to the porch.

Are you Abe?

Abe nods. Where's Heza?

Who?

Abe doesn't want to say again. The man looks into the house. Abe walks into it.

There's people in here too. There's never been so many people in the house, never more than their mother and him and Heza, and maybe a friend. Jude or his friend Elm who's off at summer camp.

The laundry basket is on the table. It's empty, which makes Abe stop. He was supposed to put the laundry away. Maybe Heza put it away. Maybe she's doing it right now. His blue shirt should be clean now. He listens for her upstairs, but there's no sound coming from up there.

His mother's keys are on the table too. On the keychain are red plastic lips and the large silver coin that the bank gave away to everyone who opened a savings account. he'd really wanted one, and his mother kept saying you can't spend the coin—the coin's not real.

I *know*, he'd say. I'll just try.

Even if you try, she'd say.

I'll just try.

I just don't want you to be disappointed.

He thought it would be funny to stroll into a store, stroll right up to the counter. Can I help you? the cashier would say.

Then he'd reach into his pocket or from behind the cashier's ear, and set the coin on the counter.

I'll take the whole store, he'd say.

The cashier's face would be so surprised.

You heard me, Abe would say, I'm buying you out. Then he'd push the coin forward with one finger.

Hey.

He looks up from the keychain coin.

Hey, he says.

Heza stands in the kitchen doorway. She has one hand on her earlobe, twisting her earring.

64

On the living room wall above the couch hangs a painting of flowers by a window. It's in a brass-looking plastic frame. Their mother brought it home from the thrift store before someone could buy it.

Our first real painting, their mother said.

The twins looked at it.

One day, we'll get a nicer painting to put there.

Maybe she thought Abe and Heza didn't hear her.

One day, she would say, low, as though to herself. But they heard, and now they can hear her saying it as they look at the painting today.

One day.

They look at each other.

They wonder if the other is hearing her too.

Behind them, voices crackle on the emergency workers' walkie-talkies.

Where'd you get that hat? Heza says to Abe.

Abe doesn't answer. He thinks she's talking to someone else.

Hey. She reaches over and tugs on the brim. He looks up at her fingers. A little rain splashes on her arm. She wipes it against her T-shirt, but that's wet too, from standing out in the rain, waiting while the neighbor ran back to his house and called the ambulance and all these other people now moving from the front of the house to the backyard.

Circus, Abe says.

Never seen a circus hat like that before.

From one of the workers. Was helping them raise the fence.

The orange one?

Yeah.

Were they going to pay you?

Didn't say.

You'll need to give it back.

He nods.

Do you remember who gave it to you?

He doesn't, but he nods so she won't be mad.

I wish everyone would go away, he whispers.

She nods.

When will they?

Soon, she says, but she doesn't know.

Then their grandmother is coming through the door, twisting her head this way and that way, starting to go up the stairs, then coming back down; then she's in the living room, searching like she's never been in the house.

Your mother, their grandmother says.

Out back, Heza says.

Heza, their grandmother says.

In the garage.

65

When their grandmother returns, the twins look into her large, wet eyes. Her cheeks are slack. Her T-shirt is embroidered with flowers in watering cans.

She opens her arms.

The children lean against her, letting their faces rest against her breasts.

She holds them against her, a hand on each of their backs, between their shoulder blades, what her daughter has somehow knowingly left behind.

Who did this? Who would do this to her Kae? She imagines a stranger knocking on the door. He's holding a fist of balloons. Kae answers, door partly open as she looks out. Buy a balloon? he says.

But wasn't Kae at work? She just talked to Kae on the telephone last night. They'd decided to watch the circus parade together, and if it was raining, they'd watch from inside the thrift store. Nice big window to see through or lean against, depending. She was on her way there when Heza called. Grandma? Yes, Heza? Mom, she...

Kae's mother imagines the man with balloons pushing open the thrift store door. The bells clank.

What do Heza and Abe know? She wants to ask. And what about that last boyfriend of Kae's? Had he been coming back around? Or had he never left?

How could this be?

With two children?

In *that* garage that Kae couldn't have trusted not to collapse as she let herself go.

On the *very* day that the circus was coming?

Not Kae.

Not her Kae.

No.

66

The twins' grandmother tells them to go pack for spending the night. Pajamas, toothbrush, tomorrow's clothes. They look up at her, their chins tipping back to look at her, their arms around her.

Go on, she says. I'll stay right here.

Heza's lip quivers.

Abe looks down.

I promise, she says.

They let go of her, leaving wet impressions of their bodies on her shirt. They take the stairs side by side. Upstairs, they sit on their beds. Much later she comes up to find them at the window, looking down.

Their grandmother steps over toys and blocks and scatterings of slick-covered books. She searches the closet for their overnight bags. Usually, they stay over weekends. But she doesn't see the bags. Her daughter knows where they are. Now, her daughter doesn't know. Because she's dead. In the garage. Hopefully, someone has lowered her. She remembers Kae climbing trees. Get down from there! Or Kae's father reaching up, lifting her down.

Her Kae, if she did it, would do it in a tree. In spring. A beautiful white flowering tree like the one Kae had stood in front of at her last birthday.

Smile, she said to Kae.

Kae smiled.

She took a picture. Should she not have told her to smile? Why didn't she ask Kae what she was thinking instead?

Do you know where your mother keeps your overnight bags?

Heza lowers herself to the floor and peers under her bed. She pulls her bag out and several dust bunnies. She stares at them. Presses the balls of dust with her thumb.

What happens next? Abe says.

There will be a funeral, Heza says.

And they will put her in the ground, Abe says.

Don't talk like that, their grandmother says.

Isn't that right?

Yes.

Because she's dead now.

Did you pack your toothbrushes?

We have some at your house.

That's right. That's right, we got them last time at the store.

The children and grandmother remember standing in the superstore aisle, their grandmother snapping her fingers, because they needed toothbrushes for her house. She let them pick out whichever they wanted. Abe's is Batman. Kae's is bamboo because it's better for the environment. Not Kae. Heza. Heza's toothbrush is bamboo.

Who built the garage where she did this? It seems important now. Who measured out the boards? Who held the nails in his teeth before hammering them in? Who did this? Who let it slump as the years passed? Who saw the holes coming through the ceiling and turned away?

68

Or the trees? Where did these trees come from that the boards were hewn from? What rivers carried them to the mill? What fish swam beneath them? What red leaves turned in the river as the logs floated down it? Who leaned over the bridge, watching the leaves pass by the logs that became the garage behind this house? Who mixed the paint to cover the wood? Did they buy it at the hardware store in town? Was that when the store opened every day? Is that where she bought the rope?

Who planted these trees?

What's rope even made from?

Who planted these trees?

Who took this beautiful tree down? Was it a beautiful white flowering tree once?

Let it be.

69

Where did her death come from?

70

Where did your death come from, Kae? Have you been carrying it since you grew inside your mother, growing inside her own mother?

Was that it?

What was it like, Kae?

Kae?

Kae's mother thinks of the birth. Thinks is too heavy a word, though. She is not thinking. Her mind has found a trillion broken pieces of glass and is picking each one up, cutting her fingers as she holds one into the light, then another, and she's like the light forced into, and through, each blue piece, each purple, each glittery gold glass. Where does glass come from?

Kae, squalling baby in the night corners of the house, and she would hold her, rocking, rocking. You're safe, she would whisper, rubbing Kae's small back, touching her fingertip to Kae's nose, brushing her finely made eyebrows. But on and on Kae would cry. And on and on her mother would rock, nursing her, not nursing her, singing through the songs her mother, and her mother's mother, sang in dark corners as young mothers.

Kae, in a purple dress and white stockings, lifting the skirt over her head, pressing the fabric against her face. Where am I? Where'd I go?

There you are! her mother would exclaim.

Kae, giggling.

Kae, sitting on the floor with a box of pencils, lifting a pencil in both hands, then pressing her thumbs against it until it snaps. Then she reaches for another. And snaps that too. Because the kids were mean at school. That's all she could ever gather from Kae. The kids were mean.

What did they say?

Words, Kae says, scowling.

What words?

Are you going to make me go back there?

To school?

Kae stares.

It's the rules that children go to school.

So you are making me? Kae says.

I guess so.

Fine. What if I break my leg like a pencil?

We'll have to go to the doctor.

Would I have to go to school?

Yes.

Kae in the circus bleachers, shoes dangling. The music's loud, and she covers her ears, but is smiling.

We need a volunteer! Frank cries into the crowd.

Anyone? Anyone? A volunteer?

Kae shoots up her hand, standing, jumping, trying to reach her fingertips above all the hands in front of her. But she is not called on, and returns to covering her ears. She doesn't seem perplexed at not being chosen.

73

But if Kae didn't do this herself. If she didn't, then what memories would come? How does death, the way of your death, summon memories for the story of who you were?

If that boyfriend of hers…

Which one? Any of them?

Kae's mother lines them up in her imagination, then knocks them down like dominoes.

She had tried to raise Kae with confidence, but she had no pattern or template.

She thinks of Kae's childhood best friend, Whit. Whit doesn't know yet. Whit will know what to do. She'll fly home. She'll take the kids to the circus. Or away from the circus. Hiking, maybe, out at Fox Ridge. Or to the mall, just wandering it for hours and eating pretzels.

Whit can help me pick out the casket.

Kae's clothes.

Whit, who never wanted to wear a jacket when it was cold outside. But Kae's mother would insist and zip Whit into one of Kae's.

Where did your death come from?

75

Kae, pay attention.

Along the ditches grows Queen Anne's lace. Foxtails. All the green and yellow weeds. The pebbles lining the roads are gray and red and orange and white. Black tar. Black bugs. Power lines cross above their shadows on the roads. That is a beautiful sky. Kae will not see it. She would have thought it was a beautiful sky. There's a house. Another field. This wasn't enough for her. Or it was. But not at that moment. What makes for a moment? This road will meet another road, and that road turns this way or that way. Over bridges. Over creeks awake and creeks dried up. The roads go the ways they always have. And a new road, though there is no such thing anymore, a new road will go the way it does.

77

If she'd…

    Then…

    But she didn't.

    So.

If she was at the thrift store only just moments ago, but her body's here.

Then…

79

She didn't only cry as a baby. She babbled. She chewed the cloth circus mobile her mom made her. She crawled. She wet her diapers. She walked. She pointed at the words for the world she knew.

School.

Math homework.

Concerts.

Field days.

Learning to swim, her shadow like a mermaid's beneath her.

She wanted to learn how to play the trumpet, but the trumpet seemed like such a loud instrument. One that would rouse a father from a growling hangover. What about the clarinet?

Kae wrinkled her nose.

And her mother knew, didn't she, that Kae didn't want to play the clarinet—or the flute—or the French horn, which is quieter than it looks.

The trumpet. *This*, Kae said, holding the demo trumpet the music store had brought to the school that spring before fall band.

But the clarinet is what her mother found at a resale shop and brought home, along with a packet of reeds the music shop man said she'd need.

And Kae took the clarinet. She learned how to play it. Learned how to read music. She sat in the row with the other clarinets and the flutes, and she tapped her foot against the gym floor during basketball games and against the stage floor at spring concerts.

But she hated the clarinet.

And after three years of band, she quit.

If she'd let her play the trumpet…

80

Heza and Abe sit in the back of their grandmother's boat of a car. A box of tissues sits on the floorboard. Heza bumps it with the toe of her shoe. Probably Grandmother doesn't know the radio's on. She's waiting for the two to buckle in. They're buckled in, but she's forgotten that's what she's waiting for.

Abe's crutch leans alone in the front seat, where Abe buckled it before climbing into the backseat with Heza. He is not aware of it, but he has stayed an arm's length from Heza since he crossed the circus field, and they stood in their backyard, standing still, watching as their mother was lifted and rolled away.

What about our car? Abe says.

What about it? says their grandmother. She's not crying, but her face is pulled down like she has been.

We can't leave it here, Abe says.

It's probably okay for tonight.

Someone could steal it, Heza says.

Abe imagines this.

Someone could steal it, Heza says again, louder.

No one's going to steal it, their grandmother says.

Someone could, Abe says.

No one will, their grandmother says.

How can you be sure?

Their grandmother starts to say she's pretty sure. But how can she know anything now? It's late afternoon. The circus is here. Kae is dead. If the sun never rose or fell again, she wouldn't be surprised.

Might not even notice. What's surprising is that both will happen, on and on. On and on.

What would her own parents have said?

She turns the key and reverses out of the driveway. She lets the car carry them up the street to the house where she has lived her entire adult life, the house where Kae grew up and lived until the kids were born. Twins.

Twins, Mother.

Twins.

Never would have guessed.

Oh my God, Mother.

Twins.

Two heartbeats.

I didn't know what the doctor meant. He said, I hear two heartbeats.

Twins.

How will we do it? Kae said.

Carefully, and the best we can, her mother said, stilling her face from the panic she felt growing inside her like a cornstalk spiraling up to the sky.

Okay.

Carefully, and the best we can.

81

Their grandmother's house is only a few blocks away, and it looks the same, but it looks like a picture of itself too. Part of the scenery for someone else's life.

She pulls into the driveway.

Abe unbuckles his crutch.

Heza kicks the tissue box one last time.

Their grandmother wonders whether she should go to the grocery now or wait until the kids have settled in. Maybe she should take them with her. No, word's getting around by now, and the grocery will be full of whispers and plain voices that reach out to her. I just heard. My God.

The kids don't need to hear that.

Or do they?

Better to go later. Disguised maybe as Audrey Hepburn. Big sunglasses and a scarf. Kae would laugh.

But Kae doesn't laugh now, her mother thinks without thinking. Because Kae is light inside shattered glass.

Just passing through, friend, she imagines Kae saying. It's a joke, Mom.

How can you joke at a time like this?

Kae's mother gets out of the driver's seat and follows the children across the driveway and up the stairs to the front door. The TV's on inside. Her husband is there. He doesn't know yet. He knows there's been an accident of some kind. But he doesn't know yet. She will have to tell him. He wasn't in the room when Heza called. And now she's back. Her body was here. Then at Kae's. Now it's back here. Like Kae's body. At the thrift store, then home, and now in a cargo van driving to the morgue in Effingham. Should she be in the van with Kae? If she were there, beside Kae, would Kae somehow feel her presence and come back to life?

Like you hear people do, come back to the light.

Over here, Kae. Over here. Feel me here like you must have felt my heart beating around you as you grew inside me.

Stop it, she thinks. These thoughts are making it worse.

Not possible.

I have to tell him, she thinks.

The children pull back the screen door, then push open the big door. The TV's louder.

Here's her husband, sitting bare-chested in his trousers and suspenders, in his recliner in front of the TV. Kae bought him the recliner at the auction a few years ago, for his birthday, or maybe Father's Day. Kae and Ada helped move it from there to here. Even Ada's ex helped. Did Kae's boyfriend? So many things she used to think were not for the better now seem exactly right. Kae should have played the trumpet, then stayed in the band and earned a scholarship to the university. A university so far away that she would have left for the dorms before the circus came that summer.

Stop thinking like that, she thinks. That story blames the children. It's not their fault.

But at least something that led to something other than this. Kae, *this* was not for the better.

My husband doesn't know our daughter's dead.

Why are you making me tell him, Kae?

Our daughter's dead.

The children, Kae's children, go up to either side of the recliner, leaning their shoulders against his bare arms.

He looks up at them. What are you two doing here? That's a surprise.

They look at him.

Mom's dead, Abe says.

The old man looks at his grandson. Then at his wife.

She gently touches the grandchildren's shoulders as she walks between the old man and the TV.

Kae? he says.

Kae, she says.

His mouth is shaped like how? But without sound, he opens his arms and she leans into him. He braces his feet against the floor to keep the recliner from tipping the both of them.

The children have never seen their grandparents embrace.

The old, faded tattoos on their grandfather's arms stare off.

It's so quiet, even with the TV, somehow. So quiet.

Their grandmother presses her cheek against their grandfather's head. He makes sounds against her arm.

Heza backs up until she's standing beside the card table where her grandmother, and sometimes her mother, works jigsaw puzzles.

That's when Heza's bladder lets go, and the warm rush of urine leaves her, washing down her leg, filling her shoe, soaking into her sock.

82

Their grandfather cleaned the splotches of pee off the stairs after his granddaughter climbed upstairs for the bathtub. Now he has left for somewhere, anywhere, leaving the roll of paper towels on the last step.

Their grandfather said Abe couldn't come with him.

Where are you going?

Somewhere.

Where?

I don't know. You stay here. Take care of your grandmother, your sister. You're the man of the house now.

I thought I already was.

Their grandfather paused. That's right. Even more so now, though.

The bath's running, and their grandmother's helping Heza remove her clothes.

I don't need a bath, Heza says.

You're covered in pee, Abe says. Abe sits in the hallway outside the bathroom door.

A bath will help, their grandmother says.

Abe hunches over his knees and traces a fingertip along the grain of the wooden floor with his fingers. The grain becomes wise men, pterodactyls, their mother carrying a laundry basket.

Heza pulls her arms out of her swimsuit and lets her grandmother tug it down her hips. She holds her grandmother's shoulder as she lifts one foot, then the other. Her grandmother tosses the cutoffs into the laundry basket. They land with a thump, thick with rain as they are.

She's dead, Heza says.

Abe whimpers.

Yes.

Two deep lines crease the sides of their grandmother's mouth so she seems like a ventriloquist puppet. Deep wrinkles. Deeper now, probably, she thinks. Her own mother had them too. Kae might have. But we'll never know. That's a different world.

A bath will help, their grandmother says.

Abe and Heza like this bathroom. The walls are tiled in white ceramic bricks. Heza usually runs her palm across them when they spend the night and take turns showering before bed.

After your bath, you can have a nap. When you wake up, maybe we'll order a pizza.

Can I go with grandfather to pick it up? Abe says.

If he's back, I don't see why not.

Oh, yay! Abe says. Then he remembers his mother's dead.

Heza stands naked in the bathroom. Maybe the door should be shut. Heza's got hair down there now. When did that happen? Maybe her brother shouldn't see that.

Can I take a bath too? Abe says.

Probably should, Heza says. Cold from the rain. All his clothes are damp from being out in that field.

Heza scoots back in the bathtub. Abe strips down and climbs in before their grandmother can say that maybe he should take a separate bath.

Their grandmother sits on the lid of the toilet and picks a sponge up from the basket on the floor. She gently pushes the sponge into the bathtub water, bubbles crinkling, and brings up the warm water onto the children's skin.

She thinks of Jesus and the women who bathed him. Baptism. Her own baptism as a young girl in a dirty creek out by the country church.

Kae's dead.

The preacher cradling her in the bend of his elbow, telling her to give him her weight.

Kae's dead.

She leaned back and closed her eyes, crossing her arms, and he laid her under the water.

You are saved.

Amen.

My daughter. My Kae. Kae, where are you? Kae.

She reaches under the sink and takes out the children's tear-free shampoo. She carefully squeezes a drop into one palm and cups one child's head, then the other, working the hair gently, pressing her fingertips against the sturdy aliveness of their skulls and grief.

Someone will need to wash Kae before the funeral.

83

Jude begins to juggle as she walks away from Heza's house. It's coming on late afternoon, which means her father will be here soon to pick her up. The sidewalk is tilty from tree roots and time. Grass and white clover grow here and there. Maybe she'll go to the church. If it's open, she'll wander along the pews or have a chat with Jesus until the secretary comes out and asks if she needs help. Probably someone's praying in there about the circus, the village, all who enter the field's chasm of sin. She could sit beside that someone.

How heavy Jesus's body must have been on that cross.

Is it blasphemous to think that?

She must have been at Heza's a while. The house was hotter than hot because the windows were down to keep the rain out. Did Heza's mom shut the windows before walking into the backyard?

Jude vaguely remembers Heza and Abe leaving, but didn't feel time passing until a policeman stooped in front of her. Hey, he said.

She looked up.

Are you Heza?

She examined his face.

Do you live here? he said. Heza?

She felt unsure but could tell he was trying to be gentle.

The walkie-talkie on his shoulder went crackly, and he stood up and talked into it, his mouth turned away from her. He was tall. She imagined his head going through the ceiling, through the roof, all the way into the rainclouds. She would climb him until she reached the sun.

Excuse me, he said, then left the room. Jude examined the dining room table. She'd eaten there. Her mom and Heza and Abe and their mom. Kae. And then after dinner, maybe a birthday cake, pie, or a round or ten of Yahtzee.

You have that memory, she thought. But that doesn't make you Heza.

You aren't Heza, she thought.

You aren't Heza, she thinks.

She juggles. She walks. She is not Heza.

I'm not Heza, and Abe is not my brother. Heza and Abe are spending the night at their grandparents' house. Their mother is dead. Will they live at their grandparents' house now? That would make them a block closer to her apartment. She feels glad, then guilty for feeling glad.

I'm not Heza.

The circus is still opening tomorrow.

Maybe she shouldn't go. What will she tell her dad? He'll understand.

Maybe no one should go to the circus. How could anyone go to the circus tomorrow?

Maybe the whole circus should be cancelled. How is a circus cancelled?

She could draw a sign, maybe, and paste it up on the village buildings. She'd have to draw more than one sign. And she only has the Elmer's Glue that she and Heza paste on their palms when they're bored, then let dry and pull off in layers like skin.

Maybe I'll steal the elephant or dig up the other one's bones, glue them together, and stand it in front of the entrance. I'll sit in a lawn chair. Nothing to see here, folks. No circus tomorrow, next summer, or ever again.

Who elected you king of the village?

That's really beside the point, now isn't it?

Someone will call the police on her for shutting down their fun. The police car will pull up, lights flashing, but no sirens since the policeman agrees there can't be a circus, but he has to answer every call. So. Here we are.

Even if she blocks the entrance, some people will just wait until dark, sneak to the back corners, and climb the fence.

And, of course, stopping people from entering the circus won't stop the circus from flipping on its lights and calling out to everybody to step right up!

So.

If Jude goes to the diner, her mom will want to know what happened.

Like, how do you mean?

What happened?

I don't know.

Jude's coming up on the funeral home with its tasteful gray paint and solemn lamps. Its gravel parking lot, though, is shabby. More dust than gravel. She sits down on a concrete parking block. She stretches her legs, her shoes skidding through the gravel. It's a familiar sound. So she does it again.

She lets the tennis balls roll from the tops of her thighs to her knees. She tries to make them roll down to her ankles without falling off.

She wishes Heza were here. Now she'd go to the pool. If Heza asked, absolutely. Even if the circus men come and Ada makes a fool of herself. Or maybe her mom just wants somebody. Is that too much to ask?

Is it? Ada will say sometimes, especially after another breakup, when she's red-eyed and the guy suddenly seems better than sliced bread.

Jude will never get married. She plans, in fact, on never falling in love or bringing strangers into her house where her daughter sleeps down the hall.

Across the street is the wide grassy lot where a house used to be. White clover grows there too. She isn't old enough to remember the house, but her mom says it was haunted. She imagines where a porch might have been. Windows. A door. Two, three floors. She imagines Kae inside, looking out.

She raises her hand to wave at Kae's ghost.

It feels very different when you know the ghost.

She rests her forehead on her knees.

84

The last time Jude talked to Kae was when she took a bag of Ada's clothes down to the thrift store. Kae took it, then said, Jude, I have just the thing for you and your juggling act. Jude followed her to the women's circular coatrack. A foam head sat there, wearing a glittery turban. Kae lifted the turban down and slipped it over Jude's head.

Look, Kae said.

Jude looked into the mirror.

What do you think?

85

The twins follow their grandmother into the guest bedroom. They're damp from the bath and forgot to pack their pajamas, so they're wearing their grandfather's white T-shirts, which reach their knees.

The sheets are clean and feel good. The pillows are soft.

So soft, Abe says, sighing.

Heza says nothing, just feeling the agreement between her head and pillow.

With the curtains shut over the window, the light is low. Their grandmother kisses them and shuts the door behind her. Their grandmother goes down the stairs. Heza tries to hear the kitchen clock from up here, but she can't.

This was their mother's bedroom when she was a little girl.

Abe lies on his side. He's crying softly.

Heza lies on her back.

Like the elephant, Abe says.

Heza doesn't answer.

Like the elephant, right, Heza?

Heza closes her eyes.

The elephant that stood on its trunk until it died. That elephant.

Heza squeezes her eyes shut as hard as she can, until colors burst in her brain. Blues and oranges. She begins counting down from sixty. Before she reaches zero, Abe's quieter. Then he's all breath. She reaches out and touches his shoulder. He doesn't respond. She holds her hand above his mouth to feel him exhale. He does, warm against her palm.

He's alive. So she turns back to her side for a while, listening to her grandmother making phone calls downstairs.

I need to tell you about Kae.

Yes.

No, not at all.

She did it.

Yes.

Earlier today.

The phone clicks. The page of the address book turns.

This is.

Yes.

Kae.

At home.

Herself.

Yes.

Heza dozes in and out of phone calls. Stay awake, she thinks. Abe is deep in it. She needs to stay awake. In case something happens. Whatever that might be.

That's kind of you to say.

Thank you.

I'll call back when I know more.

Goodbye.

About Kae…

Earlier today.

I appreciate that.

It's hard.

We feel numb right now.

Yes.

I'll call when I know.

A total shock. But isn't that the understatement of the year?

Heza sticks one leg out from under the comforter. Then the next. And slides slowly from the mattress to the floor. She rummages through the backpack for clean underwear before tiptoeing across the room to the door, then down the hallway, the stairs. The dryer's thumping with her and Abe's wet clothes. She picks up the red boots and carries them with her out the door.

Outside, at the end of the walkway, she hesitates.

What if Abe wakes up and finds her gone, then kills himself?

For the rest of her life, she will hesitate. For the rest of her life, every person she dares to love she will imagine coming home to find dead.

Heza starts walking. What else is there to do but walk on the day your mother dies? She has no idea. It's never happened before.

86

They're talking in the park. The grocery store. The diner. That house, and that house. Over clotheslines, across backyards. At the end of each row of corn. On the grain elevator scale. From one kitchen telephone to another. Two cars meet in the middle of the road and roll down their windows.

Oh my God.

Why'd she go and do a thing like that for?

Who?

Kae.

Kae?

That can't be right.

She had everything to live for.

Guess not.

Those poor children.

Didn't she know it?

Do the kids know?

Girl twin found her.

Lord almighty.

Seems fishy.

Where's she now?

It's not gonna make me the popular guy, but the Bible says what it does about suicide.

I mean, where's the girl now, and her brother?

Not Kae.

Kae?

You're thinking of someone else. Kae's the one who worked at the bank, and now the thrift store.

When's the funeral?

No one knows. Three or four days is my guess, but that's for the typical way. Don't know if her way of doing it changes anything.

Kae?

Do the children know?

Two or three children.

On a cold-case show, a husband staged his wife's murder to look like a suicide.

That's Hollywood.

This wasn't Hollywood. Town just like this.

When the baby came stillborn, her mother called us up to come get the baby shower presents we'd gotten her. Thing is, the gifts were unwrapped and set up in the nursery. We had to get them from there.

Kae never had a stillbirth.

Kae? I thought you said Cade.

Terrible thing to happen.

Terrible.

Circus time is supposed to be the best time. Nicest time. And now this.

At least the kids can still go to the circus. Might help take their minds off it.

Things like that don't happen in places like this.

Until they do.

Those poor kids.

Abe and Heza.

Heza and Abe.

Kids bounce back from this stuff. Don't get me wrong. It's hard, but it's lucky they're twins. They have each other.

And their grandmother.

Yes, and grandfather. So not so bad.

It's bad.

Could be worse.

Could be better too, couldn't it?

The botched ones.

Some people live through it, but their brains aren't ever the same.

It's not like the soap operas.

Heza and Abe.

Abe and Heza.

What kind of mother?

Imagine how hard it must have been on her to leave her children like that.

Kae sat beside me at the last pancake supper.

Heza's just a kid.

It's happening younger and younger. Kid age six, saw it in a newspaper.

Jesus.

Not Heza. Kae. Heza's the daughter. When I was living in Texas, I had a neighbor. Nice girl. She and her husband lived down the street. Nothing seemed amiss, nothing anybody could point to, but I just had a feeling he was hurting her.

Do you know how many women die by strangulation? You won't believe it.

I don't even know what to say.

Choking doesn't leave marks. Like concussions.

That NFL player who wound up homeless and killed himself.

Because of all those concussions.

I don't know how anyone can still watch football, knowing that.

Think of all the behaviors that, even five years ago, had no causes.

Except maybe the devil.

There's always that.

It is what it is.

Maybe she got hurt by some boyfriend, maybe far back as high school.

Maybe she fell out of a swing enough times as kid, or hard enough, that her death is an effect of that, from way back.

Maybe she dove off the high dive but didn't protect her head.

Maybe she suffered from depression.

You know how her father drinks.

Good guy, though.

I'm just saying.

No marks? So how could you even prove it?

Maybe a depression just swept over her, like one of those huge waves that kills thousands of people all of a sudden.

Maybe.

Maybe this isn't kosher, but isn't hanging a man's way to do it?

Is that how she did it? I hadn't heard. But I didn't want to ask either.

A woman can't even hang herself without people judging her method.

She was always kind of a strange one.

If she'd died in a car wreck, you wouldn't be calling her strange.

Strange people die in car wrecks too.

I'm just saying.

That Tammy's daughter? Tammy and Roy's?

You don't get over a thing like that.

Where are the children now? Anybody seen them? I can't imagine.

You think you know people.

A place like this.

She was a late-in-life baby, wasn't she?

Her poor parents.

You never get over a thing like that.

Are they sure it was suicide? Couldn't it have been an accident?

Or foul play. I mean, right when the circus comes in?

I'll put her parents' names in Sunday's bulletin.

I didn't know Kae had depression.

Plenty of people kill themselves who don't have depression.

Is that true?

Just saw her the other day at the thrift store. She helped me find a teapot. I'd priced them at the superstore, then thought I might find one at the thrift store, and lucky me.

My boys were with Abe when he found out. That's how I found out.

Was there a note?

Right in the mid-morning. Think about that.

Did she go to work today?

She did. I saw her watching the circus come in.

But she died at home?

Guess so.

I never have trusted the circus.

What's the circus have to do with it?

A soldier doing it makes sense.

The terminally ill.

Teenagers. Hormones all akimbo.

But Kae?

It's really not that bad living here. Maybe as a kid I didn't like it so well, but it's different the older you get.

87

Like my friend Joan's son who hasn't been right since that last tour. How Joan worries. I shouldn't say this, but sometimes I wish he would because it's like she's mourning him alive. Who he used to be, who he is now.

I took in what was left from Mom's estate sale. Kae helped me carry the boxes in. She asked after Brady like she always does. I told her he was getting married. Maybe I shouldn't have. What with her not having a husband. Happiness isn't always good for people, you know, when it's someone else's, anyway. You know she and Brady dated a while.

But she asked about him. I never talk about Brady to Joan's son. Brady wanted to go into the service, but, you know, his foot. He's lucky, even if he doesn't think so.

His fiancé works at a preschool. Hopefully, they won't wait too long. A baby's always nice. Takes your mind off the hard stuff. Though she might be one of those who will insist on working, like it's a Girl Scout patch. Of course, more women do now. I'm thankful Sam had a good job.

Kae, now, she never had that option. But she didn't complain either, and I respected that. Once when I watched the twins while she and Brady went to a movie, afterward she insisted on paying me. I wouldn't allow it, of course, but she sure meant it.

It didn't work out between them, but the odds weren't good. He tried. She tried. But the twins were three or four at the time. Brady has a big heart. She and those kids always had a special place in my heart, even after the breakup. He wanted to invite them to the wedding, and I said, Think more on that.

But what can anybody tell from looking? There's millionaires that drive junkers. I saw a program. Fenders falling off. These men you'd never imagine were millionaires, at least until you saw their wives. Sam called it trading up. Have you heard such a thing?

The point is, it's a real shame about Kae. She wasn't bad looking. But you never can see inside a person's head.

There's shadows, no matter where you point the flashlight.

88

Just the other day, I read in the paper about a man doing it the same way, in a park right in Chicago, and nobody noticed him all morning, just walking past, under him, somehow. How can you miss a thing like that? Terrible. I just. Imagine. I mean. This world. All those people jogging by. Sunny day. And a man right there.

Oh, Kae.

Sweet Kae.

Heza found her.

Can't unsee a thing like that.

Someone needs to tell Perry, if they haven't. Wasn't he our last class president when we graduated? Class will want to send flowers like they did at Freddy's funeral. It meant a lot to Jan. How many of us are left now?

90

Not everything's about that.

Could be something *like* that, and people are killing themselves because of it, but nobody understands the actual pattern.

An environmental serial killer? The data required for that. I mean…nobody even agrees on cancer.

The farmers, though. There's already studies that show a rise in farmer suicides. Didn't I share that article with you?

Won't there be an autopsy?

Step right up. Cover your mouth with this mask. The elastic goes behind your ears.

Stand right there.

First, we must search for tattoos. Here is her arm. Raise it.

No rings on her left or right hand.

Lift her other arm.

Come over here. See this soft patch of skin beneath her belly button? See how it wrinkles so gently, like the tiniest of ripples in a pond? Do you know what it is? It's her C-section scar.

Roll her onto her side. Onto her chest.

Ligature marks consistent. Bruising around her arm.

Now we will remove her clothing.

Record these details. Jeans, tank top. No bra. Make a note that she's not wearing a bra since it's common to wear a bra, even if it is summer and hot. No socks. No shoes.

It would be easier to cut off her clothes, which once was standard procedure, but now families receive all items after processing. Do you understand?

Record the color of her underwear. Use primary colors, even if you'd argue those are periwinkle. Blue. The size shouldn't matter, but record it anyway, in case someone asks.

You know, it wasn't until I started doing autopsies that I realized that those matching bra and panty sets in department stores are rarely ever worn together. Here I'd spent years feeling bad when I didn't coordinate my underwear.

Don't say I didn't teach you anything.

Now we have to take her apart so that we can understand what has happened.

At her breasts, cut under and around. We do not cut through breasts.

Now, we will peel her apart at the seam. Set her ribs over here.

Look at that.

Here, take the streamers from her fifth birthday.

Take the scratches from her tabby cat when she was seven.

There's the memory of her mother's face in the rear-view mirror. See that?

Here's the memory of her father taking her out to see the old bridges. They don't make them like they used to, do they?

Here are the lyrics to every song—just weave them together for now to keep them from breaking apart. Set them in that container.

Here's the horse she drew over and over until she got it just right. Stand the horse over there, stack the drawings here.

Weigh her heart.

Her lungs.

Oh, Kae.

Look how well she hid every bit of herself—not only from her family and everyone in the village but also from herself.

Certainly, no one could have seen this coming.

92

Heza climbs the stairs to Jude's apartment.

She tries the doorknob. Door's locked. She knocks.

Maybe Jude's dad already came and got her. Maybe she's out helping at the circus. But her dad already has tickets, so Jude doesn't need to work for them.

The smells of diner food come up the stairs. Heza's stomach turns. She can't tell whether she's sick or hungry.

Her feet are sweaty in the boots. She wiggles her toes. She can feel where the lining's torn. They're too small. Mom was right.

She presses her cheek to the door. Jude? You there, Jude?

She listens into the emptiness a while more before taking the stairs down.

At the last stair, she sits, pulling the white T-shirt over her knees and down to her ankles. She watches the fabric stretch, how the threads move in tiny Vs. She looks at the stitches on the boots. She examines the stair. If she looks up, she'll see the thrift store across the street, and she doesn't want to. Not yet.

Heza leans forward, like before she pushes off the edge of the swimming pool. She can hear the park pool in the distance. Kids. Whistles. Walk. Slow down. No running. Another whistle.

People are swimming, and my mother's dead.

She twists her earring post. Her ear burns. Green goo comes off on her fingers. She rolls it into a ball, then stretches it until it breaks. She wipes it on the edge of the stair. She touches her ear again. Infected.

93

Jude isn't in the diner when Heza pauses to peer in the window. People look back. She hurries away. She watches the sidewalk for bottle caps and nickels like her mom was always doing. She wanders down the alley.

Ada and the other waitress, Trish, are in the back, leaning against the wall. Ada's digging into her apron and takes out a pack of cigarettes.

You make bank? Trish says.

It's looking good.

Ada lights a cigarette, then untwists a red-foiled candy and pushes it into her mouth.

Trish holds her cell phone at arm's length. She smiles and tilts her head. The phone makes a camera sound.

What's that for?

Trish is busy pushing buttons.

That guy I told you about.

Ada rolls her eyes.

I know, Trish says. Nothing sexier than a selfie after a long shift and another to go.

What time we meeting tonight? Ada says. Seven? Eight?

Either way, bring your swimsuit.

What's that?

Swimming after drinking, Trish says. A party for Frank, I guess.

Frank? Ada says.

That's right. Are you gonna wear makeup now that it's Frank?

You sure you aren't thinking of the circus party?

I'm sure. Circus party's for kiddies, isn't it?

Heza clears her throat.

The women look up.

Heza? Ada says.

Is Jude at her dad's? Has she left already?

You look bad, girlie.

Thanks, Heza says, but have you seen Jude?

Ada says, She might be up packing. Don't know if Davey was taking off early to surprise her, or what. Wouldn't put it past him.

I already checked upstairs, says Heza.

You want, I can text him, says Ada, slipping her phone from her apron.

Maybe she's at the circus, Trish says.

Eavesdropping on those jugglers, Ada says. Did I tell you about that?

Trish shakes her head.

Tell you later, Ada says and turns back to Heza. Heza's twisting her ears.

I'll text Davey. Anyway, I need to know which day he plans on bringing her home.

I'll go look out at the circus, says Heza.

Have you eaten? Ada says.

Heza begins backing away. I'm sure you're right about the jugglers, she says. Thanks for the tip.

Why don't you wait a bit, come into the diner, sit a spell. Jude might very well come in while you're waiting.

That's okay.

Heza, your mom…

And then Heza's running up the alley, boots clacking.

Ada shakes her head. Then takes a drag. Then rubs her hands down her face.

It's no good, Trish says.

Ada nods. The cooks are cursing inside.

I told Kae to pick up a shift. I never say that. How long has it been since she worked here, but I said, take a shift, Kae. Why did I say that this time?

We could use some help in here, the cooks call out the door.

Ada drops her cigarette and twists it under her shoe. Trish follows her back inside, screen door thwacking behind them.

94

Heza's passing by the hardware store when the door opens.

It's not her mother.

It's the hardware man's son, looking through his door keys. His father used to own the hardware store. When Heza goes to the store with her grandmother, her grandmother chats to the man who is Kae's age and she remembers when he was yay high and pedaling his tricycle around the concrete floors. And now with children of your own! Those were good days.

They were, they were.

He locks the door, and Heza steps to the side so he can pass. He nods. She nods back. He pauses.

You're Kae's daughter.

That's right, she says.

Heza, he says.

She wonders what to say. What would her grandmother say? Heza says, You going to take those sons of yours to the circus?

They've been looking forward to it, he says.

Abe has too. My brother, Abe.

I'd imagine, he says. Listen, I'm sorry to hear about your mother. And his face does seem pained. She wonders why. They've never talked to each other, maybe never stood near each other this long, even when her grandmother's talking at the counter.

Listen, he says, I should tell you.

Yeah?

I didn't sell it to her.

Heza watches his face.

I didn't sell her the…how she…you know.

The rope, Heza says.

Yes.

She thinks of the pins of light coming through the garage roof and onto the concrete floor.

When she looks up, he's already in his truck with the engine running.

95

I couldn't reach.

96

Frank sits under his camper awning. It's green striped on green. He leans back in his chair. Most of the tents are raised, entrances rolled back to let the air move around and dry the grass before the canvas floors are put in, if they even bother. Might be dry by tomorrow.

Join you? says the circus boss.

Frank looks up. Ticket booths up?

He nods and sits. Bad but not too bad.

Frank nods.

Still a pretty long line with the rain and all.

Frank and the circus boss look up the midway to where the ticket booths stand. People are lined up into the road. Some still hold umbrellas open.

A few men walk past wearing rain boots and swimming trunks, towels across their shoulders. The circus boss lifts his camera and peers at them, but he doesn't press the button. He lowers it back to his chest.

Frank says, You tired of showing the beauty of the circus?

That what you think I'm doing?

Something like that.

Circus boss looks at the back of the camera.

Frank says, You wanna go back and see her, I can hold down the fort.

She asked me to, but I don't want to. You think I'm terrible?

Frank sits there, hands folded.

You do, the boss says. Not like I can wheel her hospice bed up the midway.

Why not? Frank says.

You think I should?

Should's a bad word, says Frank.

You're so goddamn wise. Thought you'd go visit your mom to-night so you can give her another ticket she won't use.

Frank shrugs. Maybe. Nothing to see these days. Different this year, anyway. In three days, I can visit and stay a while.

If you don't go, we should go for a swim later, says the boss. Like the old days.

Frank laughs and stands up. Gonna make me a sandwich. You want one?

Not on that healthy bread.

That's all I got, says Frank. He's been on a kick lately about healthy bread. Thick bread. Organic. Multigrain. As many seeds that fit on it as possible.

Fine.

Frank climbs into the camper.

The circus boss raises his camera. The men with their swim towels are walking up the road now, nearly to the park. Good. If Frank knows anything about the party, this will throw him off.

A child comes into the lens. How's that? Nobody's supposed to get past the ticket booths right now.

Child in red boots and a white dress. Or robe, maybe.

Closer she gets, the clearer he sees her.

Her hair's cropped against her head. Not a white dress, a T-shirt. It's starting to speckle with mud like some kind of egg.

Frank comes out of the camper carrying the sandwiches on paper plates.

Looks good, says the circus boss, taking the plate.

Better than good.

The circus boss starts picking off the seeds and dropping them on the ground. He nods at the little girl, who's making a straight line toward them.

Who's this little monk? Frank says.

Heza stops at the grassy edge of what's Frank's yard for the next few days.

Hey, Frank says.

Hey, she says.

Tickets are for open days, not closed days. This is a closed day.

I know, she says.

You live around here?

She nods.

Then tell Mommy or Daddy to buy tickets.

My mom's dead.

The men look at each other.

Sorry to hear that, kid.

Yeah, she says. She keeps standing there, arms at her sides. I'm looking for Jude.

Both men look at her now. Her still face. Her small nose. The very red earlobes and the silver balls stuck into them.

Your ears hurt? says Frank.

They're infected, she says. Have you seen another girl like me?

Can't say that I have, says the circus boss.

Frank shoots him a look. Then he asks Heza if she needs to put something on her ears. Mercurochrome? Neosporin?

She looks at the sky, then back at them. Jude likes to juggle. She's about my height.

Your friend trying to run away with the circus or something?

I hope not.

You hungry? says Frank. He walks slowly up to her, holding out his plate.

I might throw it up.

When's the last time you ate? Frank says.

Breakfast, I guess. Before Mom died.

She die today?

She nods.

Shit, says the circus boss.

Watchyer mouth, Heza says.

Frank smiles. So you're the kid that saved my life this morning.

Except you weren't dead, she says.

And that your brother, too, that helped?

Yeah.

Where's he?

Taking a nap at our grandparents' house.

Frank walks over to his lawn chair and carries it to her. Have a seat, he says. And I'll go whip you up a sandwich, bigger than your head. How's that sound? Because a girl's got to eat, don't she, boss?

That's right, Frank.

You like mayo?

She looks at him.

I'll bring it on the side—how's that?

Frank feels her watching him climb back into the camper, but when he looks, she isn't. When he emerges with her sandwich, she's in his chair, looking at her hands. He half expected she'd be gone, like those stray cats that leave as soon as you stop feeding them.

But here she is. He lowers the plate into her hands, trying not to startle her. Sandwich, he says.

Damn good bread, the circus boss says.

Frank gives him a look. Boss winks. She lifts the sandwich to her mouth. They watch her like they do a sick animal that might need a veterinarian.

Frank watches her face. She watches him as she chews. She's not the first kid to wander up the midway, but she'll be the last kid he meets like this.

Your mother been sick for a while? the circus boss says.

Heza shakes her head.

She takes another bite. Frank can't tell whether it's because she's hungry or doesn't want to talk. She swings her legs.

What's your name, kid?

Heza.

Hera?

Heza.

You named after the circus or something?

That's right, she says. I'm thirsty.

You want water or wine? You're probably too old for wine.

She giggles.

Water it is. Frank starts to get up, but the circus boss stands. I'll take a turn, he says.

Your parents circus people? says Frank.

My dad worked for the circus.

That right?

What was his name?

Mom calls him a Summer Boy.

The men look at each other.

I never met him, Heza says, then leans back and stares up at the awning. What if the whole sky were made of stripes? she says.

The two men look up too.

She pokes a tomato back between the bread. Then wipes her finger on her knee. She takes another bite.

Behind her, the Ferris wheel starts turning. Frank and the circus boss start clapping hard. Clap, Frank says.

She does.

More, he says.

She claps harder.

Why? she says when they're done.

Always a miracle when that thing starts up. One day it won't, and we'll just leave it wherever that is, I guess.

Like the elephant? Heza says.

The elephant?

The one that stood on its trunk.

The two men look at each other.

You know, she says. And it's buried somewhere out here. She gestures all around her.

Hey, Frank says, you wanna ride the Ferris wheel?

She runs her tongue across her teeth. Okay, she says, and leans over to set the plate on the ground.

Whaddya say we show you around? Would you like that? Meet

the acrobats. Behind the scenes. Clowns.

Jugglers. You like jugglers?

No, Jude does.

That your brother?

My brother's Abe.

Well, we'll show you all around. Worst day of your life doesn't have to end as bad. Because we're here. Circus is here. You like the trapeze?

She watches them. Her chest hurts. Probably Abe's awake by now. She should go get him. He'd like to try the trapeze. Maybe they can run away with the circus, after all. Not tonight, but when it's leaving.

Come one, come all, and see the twins with hearts identically broken!

The hawkers stand inside their tents, hanging up the stuffed bears, unicorns, and cartoon characters from last summer's blockbuster. They unpack the fish bowls, blow up balloons for the dart game, fill the moat for rubber duckies to float, bottoms numbered to match a prize basket behind the counter. Plastic kazoos, pocket mirrors, tiny rubber aliens wearing black sunglasses, which are more popular than you'd think. No better than what's in the quarter machine at the diner, really, but the kids won't admit it since they thought they were playing for the big prizes hanging from the awning.

Right now's the last calm, last round of setup, where it's easy to forget how much money you're not making and let your mind follow the task. Nobody broke down on the way here, no animal is sick or showing it, and the rain didn't delay setup too much. Nobody's walked off, thrown a punch, kicked an animal or camper or child, and Frank's already done his walk up the midway, hands in his pockets, nodding as he goes, and that's good. Better than good. But don't say so, or you'll curse the next three days. And Frank don't seem to know a thing about the surprise retirement party the boss is planning for tonight, after last call. Reserved the whole damn swimming pool. But lie low, kids. I've been around a few times, and when everything's smooth, everything's on the verge of shattering too.

Of course, there's the village woman who offed herself today. Bad luck, but nothing to do with the circus. A hundred years ago, maybe the villagers would think so. Might wonder what magic or witchcraft the circus brought in. Spectacle has limited trust-value.

Of course, these days, the woman's death might be bad luck, but it might increase business too. The circus is a good excuse to drive into the village and past the dead woman's house.

99

It has been a long time since the old man walked into a bar.

Like a joke, he thinks as the door shuts behind him, brushing air up his back. The low light takes over his eyes. The silhouettes of objects slowly sharpen in front of him, and all becomes as familiar as his childhood bedroom.

The counter stands where it always has. The stained-glass lampshades hang over the pool tables. The few windows let in just enough light to make the darkness murky. The round tables. Stools. Cardboard coasters.

Same, same, same.

My daughter's dead.

Not the same.

He approaches the counter and lifts himself onto a stool. The stools have backs, which he's always liked.

Kae wouldn't want him there. Wouldn't want him to leave the house to begin with, leaving her mother with the grandkids to explain what's happening. And how can she? He doesn't know himself, so what use would she have for him? His wife wouldn't like him here either, but she'll understand. Hopefully.

Understanding doesn't mean liking it, he imagines her saying.

Jesus, Kae. A thing like that. He presses the heels of his hands up his face, against his eyes, shutting them.

He sees her in that garage and drops his hands so fast they hit the counter.

The bartender comes over, like he's been summoned, and seems irritated about it. No reason to knock the counter when there's hardly anybody here.

The old man gives his order.

The bartender turns, pulls down this bottle and that bottle. Scoops ice. Then he turns, flicking a coaster down under the glass. Same glass as always. Heavy on the bottom in a way that assures his hand.

Going to the circus? says the bartender.

What's that? says the old man. He knew a guy who did it. In a room by himself too. Terrible thing. Nice man, nicest man he'd ever known, and not just because he's dead now. Really was a kind man. What was his name? Had this thick, red hair that he said had embarrassed him as a kid because kids gave him hell about it. When they knew each other, he always wore a dark peacoat with busted pockets. Showed him once, how the lining was unraveled and his hands fit through it. Then the red-haired man stuffed his hands back in his coat. Never would have known about those pockets to see him standing there like that.

And now Kae. Is she sitting in a circle of people, introducing herself to the others, maybe sitting beside the red-haired man, and he's turning his pockets inside out? Would she understand? And what's she showing him? She holds out her hands, palms cupped side by side.

What you got there, Kae?

He leans against the counter as though he can see inside her hands too.

You need something? says the bartender.

Kae, he thinks. He shakes his head. He leans back.

You drive by it? says the bartender.

The old man looks at him.

The circus field.

He tries to remember the last time Kae cupped her hands and had him look close at what she was hiding, or what she'd caught.

A toad with its throat rippling?

A quarter?

Some bauble from the quarter machine?

A robin's egg, locust shell, catalpa flower, Indian bead.

A green or silver sequin from Hezada's costume. Watermelon seeds. Can we plant them? They might not sprout in dirt that's more clay than anything.

You get your tickets ahead of time? says the bartender. Seems like the only way to do it these days. Had them half off at Rural King, I heard.

Old man shakes his head. Did Kae get the twins tickets? She's always been good about that. We never were when she was a little girl. Really made it hard on her, having to work her patience until they could go on the second day, sometimes the last day, and once, they were all sold out. That was a bad time.

Me neither. Seen one circus, you've seen them all.

But the old man doesn't believe the bartender. The way he says it. Like it's a hundred years of people saying it out of his mouth.

Always seems new to me, says the old man.

True, says the bartender and looks up in the corner at a TV. That's new. There's a TV in the other corner too. Bizarre.

The bartender lifts a water glass to his lips, still watching the TV behind the man.

Always liked the tightrope walker, says the bartender. Somebody was telling me they used to do that without a net.

The old man shakes his head. Kae, in the garage. He didn't see her there, but it's there again, more vivid than memory.

I saw a woman fall once, says the old man. From way up there.

She die?

I don't know, the old man says. But you should have seen the light against her sequins as she fell. I'll never forget that. These dark blue and green sequins, like a peacock, flashing as she fell.

Damn. That must have hurt.

I caught her.

What's that? says the bartender.

I caught her. I was right there in the front row. My buddies too. We were leaving for the service the next day, and an old timer or somebody bought us all tickets to the big show. We almost didn't go because we had our own celebrations in mind. But we went, and what seats! Best any of us ever had. So close I could see cigarette burns in the clowns' pants.

You don't say, says the bartender.

So we were right there, and this was when they served beer in the tents or people brought their own.

The good old days.

Not that we needed to buy. Every time we tried, somebody behind us bought the round. Every time. We ordered, they paid, we drank. And drank. Boy, we did. More than we should've, but not as much as we did when we came home.

Vietnam?

More or less.

Thanks for your service.

The old man pushes at his empty glass. Bartender's not wearing a nametag because the regulars know him, and everyone else knows him after a few drinks. Kae probably knew this guy.

Kae liked the circus, he says.

Helluva thing, says the bartender. He refills the old man's glass.

I don't want to talk about it.

Never would have thought she'd do a thing like that. Not Kae.

Please, the old man says. But the bartender's looking back over his head, at the TV.

I saved that woman, that trapeze artist.

Thought you said she was an acrobat.

I saw her before she fell. We were so close.

Front row.

That's right. So close I could see the bottoms of her feet. She was wearing these beige slippers. Not house slippers, more like dance slippers, I guess. The bottoms were black with dirt. I'd never seen the bottoms of a woman's feet before, except my mother's. So when she began to slip, I started moving toward her. Didn't even think about it.

Because there wasn't a net.

That's right, and I was watching her feet, her balance.

Watch! Watch closely how the young man in his uniform springs from the front row into the ring, running with his arms raised. He's reaching, and the woman's falling, a mess of sequins, and her eyes. Her eyes.

Her eyes wide with the feeling of dropping, of not being caught, of not knowing he's there.

But he is. He's there, holding up his hands, palms out. And she lands right in his hands.

The old man raises his glass. He looks at his own arm. She used to be no longer than his forearm. He touches the bend of his elbow. His wrist. From there to there.

The bartender takes the glass, refills it, returns it.

Hezada, says the old man.

Hezada, says the bartender. I never know which is better. The circus or the circus stories. What do you think?

The old man takes a drink and sets the glass back down. He looks at his fingers where they hold the glass. One night, when he was putting her to bed, she grabbed his fingers with both hands and said, I like your fingers. With that sudden intensity she had. She spread them apart, examining them like she did everything as a child. Never met a child so intent on knowing what she was looking at. He pressed his hand against her face. It covered her like a catcher's helmet. She giggled. He closes his eyes, trying to hear it.

100

Why didn't you call?

Before I—?

Yeah.

Seriously?

If you'd called. You knew our phone number. Same number your whole life.

Dad, you don't even answer the phone.

Sometimes I do.

I called last night.

I mean this morning. I would've answered this morning.

You don't know that.

Don't tell me what I know.

And what would we have talked about?

What you were thinking of doing.

Wouldn't have been much of a conversation, if that's what it were about.

You would have changed your mind, maybe.

Dad…I…

At least I could have said hello. At least you could have said hello back.

And then what?

I could have said not today. It could have been a short conversation.

How would you know what I was thinking?

You could have told me.

I wouldn't have.

You could have said do you want to go to the circus? And I could have said not today, and you might have known what I actually meant. Like code. Like when you were a kid and on that kick about writing coded letters to me and your mom.

We haven't talked on the phone in years. You don't like talking on the phone.

Jesus, Kae. A call like that. Of course, if you called to tell me that.

You would have tried to talk me out of it.

Nothing wrong with that.

That's why I didn't call.

I guess. We could have talked about anything. You didn't have to say that. Maybe we would have gotten to talking, and you would have changed your mind on your own, and you wouldn't have told me about that either. The thinking and the changing your mind. People change their minds, Kae. You think, I'm going to work in the yard an hour. But then once you're out there, you stay longer, all the way to twilight because there's just a good feeling.

I would have told you the circus came in. That Heza and Abe were excited.

Yes, and maybe I would have said, on a whim, we should go together, just you and me, like the old days. Just for the heck of it, you know.

You wouldn't have said that.

If it were a whim, I would have. On a lark, like your mother says.

That sounds nice.

That's right, just you and me walking over to the circus. I'll buy you anything you want.

A light-up sword?

Sure.

A genuine pearl necklace?

Its pearls found in the deepest point of the ocean, where no living soul has dived so deep until now.

She laughs.

Absolutely, Kae. Anything, Kae. If I would have known.

And if you hadn't?

I don't know, Kae. You didn't give me the chance. What about a lemon shake-up? You always liked a lemon shake-up, didn't you? I could have taken twenty dollars out in one-dollar bills. You could have played every game.

We could have played together.

Yes.

That would have been good.

The balloon dart game.

Bowling pins.

The glasses that look like they should fall.

But never do.

No.

We wouldn't have won anything.

That's okay. Or maybe we would have.

A fish.

Two fish. As many fishes to fill an aquarium. Seen a big aquarium down at the auction house just the other Saturday. Bigger than me. So big I thought it was one of those magician tanks, the sort they nearly drown in before saving themselves.

You did not.

Sure, I did. And I would have told you about it. How we could set it up in your living room, fill it with water, get a filter for it.

Kae laughs.

See, you never would have expected that. So how could you have done that? You hadn't thought of that.

Dad.

How could you have thought you knew everything that would happen so that you could leave? You couldn't know. Nobody knows.

Please, Dad.

You don't even remember half of your life, when you was born and I'd lay you right here on my forearm because it made your belly feel better, and I'd fly you around the house, little airplane.

Please.

You loved it. You don't even remember parts of yourself, so how could you kill them too?

It's done.

If I would have known, it would have taken only three minutes to get to you.

You don't run that fast.

Two minutes.

Now you're being silly.

I'm serious, Kae. Never run as fast as I would have today. So fast I'd have woken up with charley horses down my legs for a week, two weeks.

Oh, Dad.

But it would have been worth it.

I know, Dad. I know you would have.

Would've changed the world to keep you in it.

Dad.

Don't leave, Kae. Not now.

Kae?

Kae?

Listen, we'll go to the circus, you and me, or with everybody, the twins and your mom, anybody you want. Then we'll go to the diner for breakfast, all of us, and order the biggest breakfast. Bacon, French toast, scoops of butter bigger than Heza's fists—remember her saying that? That butter's bigger than my fist!

I remember.

It'll be a good time, all of us, Kae, and you don't worry about the bill, you hear me? Breakfast's on me, so you eat as much French toast as you like. Powdered sugar. Jelly. Or whatever you want. Hashbrowns? Done. Pancakes? You got it. Full order too. None of this half-order, on-a-diet bullshit. You, the kids. We'll eat all day, we'll nap in the booths, and when we wake, we'll eat more. You hear me, Kae? It'll be wonderful. You hear me?

101

It's dark now, and more people are coming into the bar.

The bartender moves fast. Flips the tip jar, empties it behind the counter, then returns it with only a dollar inside. He reaches for the shaker, tosses in ice. Gonna be a good night. So good maybe he'll buy the circus. He smiles. He whips a cocktail napkin under the glass, sends it to its drinker, and points at another woman. She leans forward, gives her order.

So many people they're walking sideways, one line leaving, one line coming, the new people raising up on their toes to see a table or whether they should drive to the town bar, but it's probably hopping too.

Might as well stay.

Excuse me, excuse me.

Sure.

Frank! says a woman, throwing up her arms.

Sarah's her name, maybe. For a long decade, Barb would've been the better guess. Before that, Nancy. Not that he ever guessed out loud.

Look who it is, he says.

Finish an argument for me, will you, Frank? My friend here says no more elephants. I say you still have two, three elephants. So what is it?

What's that? Frank says.

Sarah pulls at her hair where it's caught in her necklace clasp.

Frank looks for a clock but can't see one. An old trick of the tavern trade.

We have one elephant, says Frank.

On the stool by Frank sits an old man talking about his daughter's first day of school. He's pretty drunk but seems nice.

I'll be right here when the bell rings at the end of the day. The old man looks at Frank. She was scared. I didn't even realize it. But the school building was so big. You remember it?

Frank nods.

So big, bigger than any building she'd ever seen. Maybe ever saw. And it didn't even occur to me. My parents hadn't walked me to school. Maybe that's why. I walked there. But she was scared. Could have carried her backpack, walked with her up the hall to her classroom. You have a daughter? he says.

Frank shakes his head.

Me neither, the old man says. He rests his forehead in his hand and shakes his head slowly. I should have nailed boards over that goddamn garage. Never was safe. Everybody knew it. Roof about to collapse any moment. I kept meaning to. No, I didn't. Just stay away from it, that's what she told the kids. And they did. They're good kids. That son-of-a-bitch landlord. But I didn't have to wait for him. Everybody knows how he treats his tenants.

You got a long drive home? Frank says.

What's that?

Looking a bit worse for the wear.

Me?

That's right.

The old man nods. Lucky for me, the beauty pageant's a few days off.

Frank chuckles.

The old man smiles.

You got a wife to call? Frank says. Or a wedding to get to?

The old man laughs this time, and Frank smiles.

Hope not.

You know somebody around here who can walk you home?

The old man shakes his head.

Look around, Frank says.

I don't know many people anymore. I'm one of those shut-ins.

That right?

That's what my daughter says.

Thought you didn't have a daughter.

I did. I do. Not sure how that works, really.

Let me help you home, Frank says.

Are you going to burgle me?

Maybe. Depends how crooked you walk.

The two chuckle together.

The old man moves carefully from the stool to the floor. There's a grace to it that surprises Frank.

My daughter's in Effingham, the old man's saying as they push through the crowd to the door. You know where that is?

Frank says he does.

Then they're out on the sidewalk.

You think you could take me to see her?

Pretty late. Probably she's sleeping.

The old man starts to correct him but then says, yes, probably she is. He's never been to a morgue. Never seen a ghost either, but he's heard enough stories to feel the fragments rising up inside him now like creek sediment in a storm.

Which way's your house? Frank says.

That's my car. Maybe I'll take a little nap.

I can walk you home. Car will be here in the morning.

Can't be too sure when circus men are in town.

Frank nods. I guess so.

I'll just have a little nap. Maybe you could drive me there.

Home?

She should be there by now. I don't know if they're in beds or drawers, though. I don't know what is and isn't like the movies.

Frank says, Everything will be better when you wake up.

The old man shakes his head. I doubt that very much. My wife will know. She'll know what to think about it. She'll tell me what we think about this. Must be late, dark as it is.

There's stars, Frank says.

The old man and Frank tilt their heads back and watch the sky for a long time. Until Frank glances over to see whether the old man's eyes are closed, if he's falling asleep like that. Then he takes the old man's hand. The old man starts to cry.

Which one's your car again? Frank says.

The old man points with his other hand.

The doors are unlocked, of course. Frank opens the passenger door. The old man climbs in. Frank buckles him in, just to be safe.

Will you sit with me a while? I feel so sad.

Thought you wanted me to drive you.

Yes, but sit with me, would you? This sadness. The old man thumps his own chest. He coughs. He sets his fedora in his lap and leans against the headrest. He's wearing brown trousers and a white button-down over a white T-shirt. Frank thinks of that girl today. Heza. Her white T-shirt.

Sure, Frank says. I've got time. Which is true. Circus boss said he'd meet up with him at the bar. Had to do a few things. Frank thought maybe talk to the woman on the phone, or at least hold the phones between them, saying nothing. What's there to say? he imagines the circus boss saying. There's only so many times you can say I love you until you're not sure if you do.

102

It's night against the windows when Abe wakes up in his grand-mother's house. He has the sense that he's dreamed. His mother's dead.

Heza?

She doesn't answer.

Heza?

She's not in bed beside him. There's a damp place on his pillow. He wipes his mouth with the sheet, then examines the tiny orange flowers in the cloth. Their centers are slightly off. He covers a flower with his thumb, but the stem and leaves still wind out through the cloth, becoming another orange blossom with a not-quite center.

The pain in his chest is still there. He pulls back the covers and looks down at his body in his grandfather's white T-shirt. It's the only kind of shirt his grandfather wears, when he wears a shirt, which is nearly never since he rarely leaves the house.

On his toenails are islands of glittery red polish from Heza paint-ing them a couple months ago. He points his toes, stretches his arms over his head, and tenses his body into an arching dive. The water is deep and dark.

Then he slides out of the bed and goes to the windows. One holds a box air-conditioner. He rests his chin on the other window-sill and looks out. The sill is gritty with dust. He touches the dust with a fingertip, then examines his finger, moving it into the light that glows off the nearest streetlight. He presses another fingertip into the dust. Another. Until he's done all his fingers. Dust is every-thing. Someone told him that once.

Stars, skin, the hollow bodies of dead flies.

A minivan pulls into the driveway. A woman gets out carrying something in aluminum foil. She disappears beneath the porch roof. There's her knock rattling the door. He waits for Heza to answer. The woman knocks again.

But it's Grandmother who moves through the house, from the kitchen to the living room. Her voice. The woman's. Then the door shuts. The woman returns to the minivan. The dome light clicks on. She turns on the car but sits with the headlights off, looking into the house. Then the dome light goes dark, and she drives away behind her headlights. The pavement's still wet from the rain.

His grandmother walks back through the house to the kitchen.

He listens for Heza's voice to ask who it was.

The refrigerator opens. A cabinet shuts. The tic-tic-tic of the stove burner lighting.

He's hungry.

He wipes his dusty fingers down the T-shirt and crosses the bedroom, into the hallway, and into the bathroom. Is his grandmother now listening to the ceiling above her?

The upstairs lights are all off. He pees in the dark, then starts down the stairs.

In the living room, the TV's going with the sound off. The recliner is empty of his grandfather, but the remote control is on the doily-covered armrest as usual. Abe walks around the old cookie tin his grandfather keeps on the floor to use as a spittoon.

The kitchen is white with light. Abe pauses in the doorway and watches his grandmother at the counter, grating a block of cheese. She is barefoot, veins netting her feet.

What are you doing, Mama? says her daughter's ghost.

This is called grating, she says.

Grading, Kae says.

Grating, her mother says, pausing to pronounce the T with special emphasis.

Kae repeats.

That's right.

Kae tilts her face against the counter, trying to see better.

Your bangs need cut, she says to Kae.

I like them, Kae says.

Can't see a thing like that. How long you growing them?

All the way the ground, Kae says.

The cheese curls against the silver blades. She pinches some and offers them to Kae. Kae wrinkles her nose.

You like cheese.

No, I don't.

That right?

That's right.

Why don't you try it?

Okay. And that's how Kae was. Disagreeable, then agreeable. Never disagreeable for long. Kae takes the cheese from her mother's fingers. A few shreds fall to the linoleum floor.

Whoops, Kae says.

That's okay, I'll sweep it later.

Grandma? says Abe.

She turns, her daughter disappearing into her grandson. He stands in the kitchen doorway. He's beautiful. Why aren't you here to see this? she thinks to her daughter.

She presses her hand against her face, trying to stop the tears before they begin again, though she feels so empty and raw from all the crying.

Let him see you grieve, Kae says.

You have no right to tell me what to do, her mother thinks. But she lowers her hand, exposing her face to her grandson. He starts walking to her.

You're awake, she says.

He nods.

How did you sleep?

Okay.

Did you dream?

He can't remember.

That's probably good, she says.

Why?

Answer him, Kae.

Don't be mad at me, pleads Kae and rushes toward the kitchen window and starts to climb out of it.

I'm not mad.

But she is.

She is and she isn't. It's not anger; a space is opening inside of her, wider and wider, like a watermelon ripening until the rind's thin as a fingernail.

Don't go, she thinks to the empty window, trying to imagine her daughter there, the bottoms of Kae's small bare feet as she climbs into the bushes to hide from her parents arguing, to hide from the drunken songs her father brought home, to hide from what else? That night or the next day, she'd pick the green bush needles from Kae's hair, shake them from the bed sheets, sweep them into the trash, gather them from the dryer's lint trap.

I'm hungry, Abe says. He rests his forehead against her arm. She touches his hair. No pine needles fall out.

Are you making dinner? he says.

She looks around. Noodles boiling on the stove. Pile of cheese on the cutting board. A jar of red sauce wrapped in the face of a smiling movie star.

Dinner, she says. Yes, I am. Go on and sit down.

Abe nods, then goes to the kitchen table. He folds his arms and rests his cheek there, watching her. The flowers on the linoleum are a different color and design than the ones on the sheets upstairs.

Is Heza still asleep? says his grandmother.

Heza, Abe says. Then he nods.

His grandmother picks up the jar and bangs the lid against the counter until she can twist it off. She pours the sauce into the saucepan. Tic-tic-tic, then the whoosh of flame.

She takes down two plates from the upper cabinet. Kae didn't like these new blue glass plates. What's wrong with them? I loved the other ones, Kae said. At least can I eat off the old ones?

I gave them away.

To who?

That doesn't matter.

Get them back.

I will not.

She carries the blue plates to the table. Abe's crying. His small shoulders shake. The T-shirt makes him seem smaller. Or the day has made him seem smaller. Or this is just his size, and everything is larger in your imagination and smaller when you look closely.

Should she hug him? Kae would hug him. What if he twists away?

She sets one plate down, then the other. She touches the back of his head gently. He doesn't yell at her.

She returns to the stove for the saucepan. She sets it on the variegated potholder that Kae wove for 4-H. She'd saved the weaving frame and given it to Heza last year, but Heza didn't seem too interested. Neither did Kae.

So why'd I save it? What am I saving any of this stuff for?

I don't know, Mom. That's what Kae had said. I don't know, Mom.

Well, you should, she had said back. There's plenty of children who would love this. Then she took the little loom back from Heza's hands.

Seriously, Mother?

You don't appreciate anything I do. I don't know why I keep doing it.

Mom.

You never have.

The house smells like garlic bread.

Abe's still crying.

Can I hold you? she says.

He lifts up his arms same as Kae when she'd help her with her pajamas.

Can you climb on the chair to help me? she says.

So he does, carefully standing on the seat.

She thinks of Kae. That chair. That garage.

Why were you barefoot? Why in that garage? Why didn't you just take a walk and never stop until you reached one ocean or another? Then we could've come got you when you were ready. Even if you were never ready, we would know you were alive. Or hoped you were. What was so wrong about taking a walk? Kae, do you hear me?

Stop it, she thinks.

She lifts him under his armpits, and bends her knees to protect her back from another injury. He wraps his arms and legs around her and cries into her neck. His tears are warm.

A car of teenagers drives by the house, honking. He flinches at the sound. She rubs his back.

More shouting teenagers drive by. The circus party.

Abe wipes his nose against his arm. A sheen of snot pastes his cheek. He rubs at it with his hand. It's bright in the kitchen.

Let's eat, she says.

I don't know if I'm hungry.

That's okay.

She sets him back on the chair. He pulls the T-shirt under his bottom. She pushes his chair in. Then she unties her apron and sits. He tries to smile at her. She does the same. She says, How much noodles do you want?

Kae raises her head above the kitchen windowsill to watch.

But not really.

If she sees us, or she imagined us like this before she did it, we should let her see we're safe. She doesn't need to worry anymore, if worrying is what it was.

103

Bar's closing, so everybody's paying tabs and moving outside to join everybody already outside deciding how best to extend the night.

There another bar around here?

One in the town, but it don't stay open much later than this one. Probably closing down by the time we get there, or just after we order our drinks.

Could take the ladies back to the camp, show them around until it's time for Frank's surprise party.

I love the circus! says one girl who has forgotten how old she is on the ID in her purse.

Who doesn't love the circus?

Camp's the last place we should go. You see Frank around here?

People look.

Somebody says, Couldn't see him if he were here.

Don't be a dick. He's not here, is he? And if he's not here, where is he?

You're saying Frank's back at camp so we shouldn't go?

That's what I'm saying, Watson. We go back there, someone's gonna let it slip or Frank'll just be suspicious since we never go back this early, and he has fifty years of routine under his belt.

What time is it?

Earlier than usual.

Frank's probably asleep.

Frank sleeps like an elephant.

You don't know much about elephants. Or Frank.

Then we might as well go to the pool now. Even if the boss isn't there yet, we can wait. Probably he is already there. He picked up that cardboard cake a full week ago.

How do you know that?

I've been hiding it in the tiger supplies, haven't I?

I forgot my goggles.

What are you gonna see in a pool after midnight, anyway?

There's always my place, Ada says. Jude's at her dad's for the weekend.

Lucky you, says another woman.

I don't know about that, Ada says.

The women lean against the brick wall. One scratches her arm. One's searching for gum in her purse. One's staring at the sky. One's holding open her compact, drawing a mouth on her mouth. Her eyes are bloodshot from chlorine or drinking or maybe it's just the lighting. There's better light from the lampposts across the street. She steps off the curb and walks into the street. She's wearing high heels that make her walk on bent knees.

Where you going?

Getting ready for my goddamn senior picture.

They laugh.

She's grabbing for the lamppost for balance.

How much she drink?

Too much.

I can hear you, she shouts.

They laugh.

She flips them off.

That's not gonna work for the yearbook.

Her friends laugh harder, leaning forward until they feel their shirts catching on the brick, then letting go.

What do you do in the circus, anyway?

He's an acrobat.

Shuddup.

Naw, he's the man on the flying trapeze. That's who he is.

Isn't that a song? I know that song. Is that a song?

What about the circus party?

That's for teenagers. You wanna go hang out with some teeny-boppers?

I don't want to stand out here all night, I know that.

We'll go to the pool. Practice our loopity-loop on the high dive.

I need to get my bathing suit.

What you need one of those for?

Ha ha. You must be one of the clowns.

Hey, can I ask you something?

Sure.

Did you get Frank a present?

Were we supposed to?

I mean, fifty years. Right?

Shit.

104

When Heza gets back to her grandparents' house, there's a casserole dish on the front porch. She picks it up. It's still warm on the bottom, and a greeting card is taped to the foil. Sympathies, reads the card in gold script. A robin sits on a branch.

Inside the house, it smells like popcorn and cookies. It's dark except for the TV. The sound's on low. Abe's in their grandfather's recliner. Their grandmother's asleep on the couch, a bowl of popcorn tilted in her lap and her head leaning back on the couch, her mouth open.

Heza shuts the door.

Abe peers around the recliner at her. What's that?

She shrugs. Meatballs or something. Somebody left it.

People been coming by all night. Thought you were spending the night at Jude's or something.

She's at her dad's, Heza says.

That's right.

What's on your face?

My face, Abe says. He wipes his hand against his mouth and examines it. Spaghetti sauce, he says. There's leftovers if you want some. Might still be warm.

On TV, people laugh, pretending to be a family.

Heza looks at the card table. The puzzle doesn't seem any more finished. She looks at the carpet for the discoloration of her pee. Too dark to tell.

Heza takes the casserole into the kitchen. There's three others in the refrigerator. She peels back the foil and lids. Macaroni. Lasagna.

Cookies. Why'd her grandmother put cookies in here? She shrugs and takes a few. There's a large case of toilet paper by the pantry and a haunting of white plastic bags from the superstore. She's surprised people drove all the way out there. That was nice of them.

Heza goes back into the living room and stands by the recliner.

Abe takes a cookie out of her hand. She lets him.

The TV family go into the kitchen. The mother leans against the kitchen sink, facing the TV. Her sister is coming in through the laundry room.

Scoot, says Heza and climbs into the recliner with him.

Circus is all set up, Heza says.

That where you been? Abe says.

Yeah.

They give you a job or something?

Something like that, she says.

He'd feel jealous if he weren't numb. It's not a bad feeling.

On TV, the pretend family chases each other around a couch.

Don't let me fall asleep, says Heza. I don't want to sleep here.

I can't sleep either.

Their grandmother snorts a snore. The twins look over at her, the embroidered flowers and pieces of popcorn on her chest.

I mean, says Heza, I don't want to sleep *here*. I want to go home to sleep.

Our home?

She nods. I want to be there in case she comes back.

Mom?

Talk softer.

You think Mom's coming back?

Heza shrugs. Maybe.

You think she's a ghost or something?

I don't know.

She could be a good ghost.

Heza nods.

On TV, a woman their mom's age stands on a dock. A man with gray hair smiles. It's for those sex pills. Their mother hated this commercial.

What if it's not true? he says.

No, she hated the commercial.

I'm talking about Mom. What if she's not dead? Like not really dead.

Heza puts her arm around him.

105

The bar group splits up with a plan to meet back at the pool. The village women didn't know to bring their swimsuits, and some of the workers are hungry and decide to drive to the university town where the fast-food restaurants are still open. We'll just pick it up and drive back. I don't want to miss Frank's party. We won't. I promise.

The people who wore bathing suits under their clothes walk to the swimming pool. Circus boss is standing at the entrance in a tuxedo jacket and swim shorts. Frank'll get a kick out of it. Boss welcomes everyone as they pass through the gates, then past him, through the dressing rooms, into the pool area.

The dressing rooms are concrete, and their laughter echoes.

One woman lies down on a wooden bench. She's drunk and sick but if she stands, the sick won't stay down.

She gonna be okay?

They're talking about her, maybe. She stares at the ceiling. It's made of corrugated metal; rectangular lights are suspended from poles.

Dunno.

You okay?

If she doesn't answer, will they keep asking?

She doesn't answer.

Don't throw up in the swimming pool.

Gross.

You remember when Todd Maxwell pooped his pants in the diving pool?

Oh my God, I haven't thought of that in years!

The woman on the bench lets her fingertips drag against the concrete floor. It's rough. She needs a manicure. She needs to go home. Her dog's waiting for her to open the door. After the diner, she went to the bar. She meant to go home between. Now she's here. Poor baby's been holding it for hours. She tries to count how many hours. Poor baby's gonna pee on the rug behind the couch, goddammit, and the internet said once an animal finds a peeing place, that's it. You could dig up your living room floor and the dog would still raise its leg there.

Ada unties her apron and pulls her polo shirt off. Its front is smeared in butter and pork-chop sauce. She worked every shift. She's got food in her fingernails, smoke in her hair.

Another woman says, You think my underwear would pass for a bikini?

What happens when it gets wet?

I so wish I could tell you the last time I got wet.

The women laugh.

Poor baby's waiting behind the front door, its eyebrows winking at any sound that might be her. How many sounds is that?

106

Heza and Abe walk side by side on the wet, dark streets. Heza in her swimsuit and cutoffs, Abe in his T-shirt and trunks. The fabric's still warm from their grandmother's dryer.

As they walk, they watch the wet flick off the toes of their shoes.

Heza in the red boots. Abe and his crutch. The crutch rattles against the screws as he brings it down alongside his leg.

Abe says, Would Mom think I'm bad for still wanting to go to the circus?

Heza laughs.

Don't laugh at me, Abe says.

She closes her mouth. Sorry, she says. I don't know why I laughed. She hugs him to her. He presses away, not sure whether to believe her.

But would she? Abe says.

I guess there's lots I don't know about her.

Yeah.

They reach the end of the sidewalk. There's no headlights coming, so they cross and keep walking. The pavement wet against their shoes. The click of the crutch.

I like your boots, Abe says.

They're too tight.

Okay.

And the insides are falling apart.

Grandpa can glue them back in, maybe.

Maybe, says Heza.

When he comes back. You think he will?

Yeah. I think he was worse when Mom was a kid, not coming home for days at a time.

Really?

Yeah.

Mom tell you that?

Heza shrugs.

She was always telling you things.

That's just the perk of being three minutes older than you.

They reach the end of another block. They look both ways. They look at each other. They walk on.

What if it was an accident? Abe says. Like maybe she was reaching for something.

And she fell off the chair?

Abe nods because the tears are coming back, and he doesn't want Heza to know.

Heza shakes her head. No, she says.

Maybe someone killed her.

Who? Like a random murderer?

Now Abe shrugs. Maybe. Nobody saw her do it. Nobody would have noticed if he snuck in while the circus was getting here. Heza?

I'm thinking, she says. I'll need to think more about that.

Up ahead, the outline of their house angles out of the dark. The porch. The bushes. Their mother's car.

Abe stops suddenly, holding his crutch up like a crossing gate. Heza runs into it. Dammit! she says and scowls. But he's looking down the row of yards. Porch light's on, he whispers. You turn it on?

No.

Me neither, he says.

They lean into each other.

Maybe Grandma before we left?

Maybe we forgot to turn it off this morning.

Maybe Mom turned it on before, knowing we'd come back.

Maybe she's in there right now.

Her ghost?

No, her.

Abe takes off running up the sidewalk, crutch stuttering behind him. Heza chases after. Wait, she's whisper-yelling. Abe! Wait!

He's cutting across their neighbor's yard to reach their porch faster, to catch their mother sneaking grapes from the refrigerator like she was last night. Did anybody wash these? their mother asked, standing up in the light of the refrigerator.

I didn't.

Abe, you wash these grapes?

What grapes?

These ones. And she held up the bag so he could see, but he shrugged without looking. The refrigerator door shut as she walked to the sink. The faucet water hammered against the plastic bag.

107

Like most every high-school party, the circus party's out on a grand-father's land, far enough into the dark and tented by enough trees to hide the twin lines of parked vehicles that lead to a bonfire and keg and a folding table laden with red plastic cups and bags of M&M's and chips.

Not that the police look hard, since they drove out here as boys, too, sat on straw bales around the fire like the boys beside these girls with their arms folded over their new breasts and the tiny crosses that hang from their necks.

The girls lean toward the fire, holding the arms of their new jean jackets.

The boys drink from their cups.

Should the girls ask the boys if they believe in God, like their church camp counselor said to? When do you even ask that? One counselor said, If it's a Christian boy, there's no wrong time to talk God.

A boy wearing his dad's boots kicks a log deeper into the fire. The fire snaps.

Watch it, says another kid.

The boy in the boots laughs. I'm not gonna catch fire, he says. He laughs again. He's big, but his laugh is high-pitched like a giggle.

Burn all you want—I don't want you to catch me on fire.

The boy giggles again and kicks at another log.

Goddammit!

Oh, calm down.

The girls think of hell. The girls wonder if the other girls are thinking of hell. When would be a good time to bring up hell? Nobody wants to be a downer. They thumb the inside cuffs of their jean jackets.

Here, a kid says as he stands. Let's move back.

The girl closest to him helps him move the bale. The wire cuts into her fingers, but she doesn't drop it because good country girls don't do that. The giggling boy giggles. She turns. He's watching the fire flicker its shadows up the backs of her legs.

She thinks, No one can see us from the road.

Don't be a downer, she thinks.

There's more boys than girls. She counts with her eyes. Stop it, she thinks.

Another girl-boy pair is talking about the circus. You going?

She shrugs. Maybe. You?

Maybe, he says.

That's cool.

It's sort of expensive, really. But I sure loved it as a kid, he says.

Me too, she says.

They smile at each other, then look at the bonfire.

Thing is, if he believes in God, she can marry him, and drive to church together and sit in the pew, his arm around her. He'll wear cologne and she'll wear good dresses and the kids will skip up the aisle for children's time and the congregation will laugh softly, and how safe her life will be. How right.

What's your favorite part? he says.

Of the circus? she says.

Yeah.

I want to say elephants, but…She shrugs. Hard to say that now I know how they've been treated this whole time.

How's that?

You know, she says, because they were in the same speech class and he heard her persuasive speech about torture as a training method. She saw him looking at her as she clicked the slides.

Hey, he says, you mad at me?

No.

Hey, he says. He bumps her. She looks at him. He's smiling enough to make dimples. Probably he believes in God.

He says, You ever go looking for that one elephant that killed itself?

She doesn't like to think about it.

He says, What's your next favorite part of the circus?

You'll think I'm weird or something.

Naw. Just pretty.

She rolls her eyes but feels a zip of pleasure. No boy's ever said that to her.

Promise you won't make fun of me? she says.

Naw, I can't promise that. He laughs. She laughs. The laugh just happens, like the village—their parents—the world—didn't raise them up to live this very moment.

He edges closer, his leg against her hip.

I like the tattooed woman, she says. The roses, she says and touches her own face, tracing petals on her forehead. Yellow and red, she thinks. Last summer, she went to the woman's show so many times she started feeling bad for going, like she shouldn't. The woman's skin like a sunlit window that roses grew against.

The boy looks into the fire. He takes a drink.

Told you, she says.

The one with drawings all over her face? he says, wincing.

What's the big deal? she says.

He squeezes the cup. It breaks.

I like tattoos same as anybody, he says. I just don't find it attractive, I guess, he says.

Nobody can see us from the road, she thinks. But she grew up here. She's fine. She'll be fine.

You want tattoos like that? he says.

You have one, she says.

It's different with guys.

Maybe she could agree if she hadn't gone to the first show. If her parents had told her what happened in the tents at the end of the midway. If she hadn't had a job, her own money. If she hadn't been the only one in the tent.

Or maybe it was the magic of the circus, she thinks. That rush when the man outside the tent took her ticket. You like tattoos? he said. I don't know, she said. Have a good time, he said. He winked and held the tent flap back for her.

Inside the tent were three or four rows of folding chairs, brown metal ones like the ones in the church basement. She sat down. She was still the only one in the tent when the tattooed woman came out. Jesus. She'd never felt like that before. And she felt it at the next show and the next and the next, always afraid she wouldn't feel it at the next show. But she did. She did!

108

The twins reach the porch of their house at about the same time.

The porch smells like it does after a rain.

There, surrounding the front door are baskets of flowers, white pots of plants. Heza mounts the porch and crouches. She reaches past the leaves of a plant to touch the tiny plastic pitchfork holding a white envelope with their names on it.

Heza and Abe.

Another envelope is addressed to The Twins.

Another envelope is for Kae's Children.

One says The Family of Kae.

Abe picks up a teddy bear whose back is stitched with silvery padded wings. There's two bears. He holds both, looking for a difference between them.

A car pulls up in front of the house.

Abe and Heza turn around.

The car pulls away slowly.

Too slowly, both Abe and Heza think. They look at each other.

You see that?

You recognize them?

Heza shakes her head.

Abe grabs her hand, tugs her to follow him as he jumps off the side of the porch just like their mother's always yelling at them not to do, liable to break yourselves, and what kings and horsemen will put you back together again?

The grass is wet and brushes against their legs.

Yuck, Heza whispers.

Abe pulls her harder, the crutch handle bumping against his shoulder.

They climb the back steps and through the back door. They tumble inside, Heza falling back to shut the door. Abe crouches down and starts crawling from the kitchen toward the living room. Heza follows.

Another car, he whispers.

Should I turn it off? she says, her hand hovering by the switch to the porchlight.

Abe glances over at her. He doesn't seem to know.

She looks out. Here comes another car, up the street. It passes their house, then stops. The brake lights flash. Then the white reverse lights. It starts rolling back until the doors are nearly even with the path up to the front porch.

You see that? Abe whispers. He's crouched on the floor in front of the picture window.

Heza nods.

The car's dome light switches on. Faces in the front seats appear, one leaning just past the other.

You know them? Heza whispers.

This time Abe forgets to speak and only shakes his head.

Someone's in the back seat.

Yeah.

The car door starts to open.

The front door still locked? Abe whispers. Heza tries it. Yes, she says.

Instead of a woman with a casserole, a girl in shorts and a T-shirt climbs out of the car and starts up the sidewalk. She seems scared. Her arms are slightly out at her sides.

Somebody lets out a scream.

The girl jumps, turning.

Laughter.

Funny, the girl says. The funniest.

More laughter.

The girl turns back to the house, starts coming toward it again.

Hit the light, Abe says.

Heza reaches fast and snaps the light off. The girl stops.

Shit! shouts someone.

Then the girl's sprinting back to the car, and it's taking off while she's shutting the door.

Abe stands, grabs both curtains and pulls them shut.

Nice work, he says.

They thought we were Mom.

Something like that.

There's the sound of crunching gravel. Heza and Abe look to the sound of it coming from the alley.

Is it the alley?

Abe nods.

Maybe this is a nightmare, Heza says.

Yours or mine? Abe says.

Heza shrugs.

Try to wake up, he says.

You too.

Okay.

Did you try?

Yes. Did you?

There's more footsteps in the gravel.

Heza opens her eyes. They want to see where Mom did it.

I'll kill 'em, Abe says in a voice so cold and sharp that the house would have lit on fire were it her nightmare, or his, and not this one where they live outside of sleep.

109

An old man wearing a felt fedora stumbles out of the woods. He walks past the folding table, the kids, the keg, and up to the bonfire. Looks like he's going to walk right into it and vanish like the devil.

But he stops, or the heat stops him. He falters. He holds out his hands, palms flat. His wedding band reflects the fire.

Well, if that isn't spooky as hell, says one kid.

Fuuuuck, says another.

Watch this, says the kid with a smile, the kid who invited everyone to his grandfather's land, to the party, the kid who basically is the party. The kid with a smile picks up two beers and walks to the old man. Wanna beer?

The old man looks at the kid, then at the cup in his hand. He nods a little, and shifts to keep balance, like moving his head's too much for his equilibrium. The kid hands him the cup. Careful now, he says. I filled it a little too high.

The old man nods.

Cheers, the kid says with a smile, and knocks his cup against the old man's. Foam rolls over the lip and down the man's fingers, splattering on the ground.

All the kids are watching. Some snicker. Some elbow each other. Can you believe that kid? What's he doing? What's an old man like that even doing here? Shit.

Love me a good fire, says the kid with a smile. Don't you?

The old man drinks from the cup.

Thanks for coming to my party, the kid says.

The old man turns as though seeing him for the first time.

Who are you? the old man says.

I'm the life of the party.

I mean...

I'm Travis, and this here's my party. Well, everybody's party. My party, their party, your party. Our party. It's the circus party. He throws his arms up. Ta-da, he says. He laughs. The guys by the keg laugh too.

You like my party?

The old man closes his eyes.

You deaf or something? You one of the circus acts or something? Travis flattens his hands against the air like he's a mime in a box or an asshole in a cornfield.

The man stumbles back. Then opens his eyes and finds balance again.

You come in with the circus, old man?

The old man tries to remember. He meant to drive to Effingham to see his daughter, but he got all turned around somehow. Or maybe he went and now he's back.

I like your hat, says Travis. He touches the short, square feather in the fedora's band.

Can I try it on? says Travis.

Travis takes the hat off the old man and sets it on his own head.

Can you believe that kid? What a party. I knew it'd be good, but... Yeah, it's good. Would be better if the ground wasn't wet as shit, but you can't have everything, can you? No, that'd be just greedy.

The kids refill their cups and return to watching.

Travis sweeps the hat from his head and stands on a straw bale. Step right up, step right up!

I've got a man with two heads, a woman with three vaginas, and more fucked up shit. Step right up!

Travis drops the hat back on his head and claps his hands.

The kids cover their mouths and hold their bellies to keep the laughter from slipping out and curling wetly at their feet. This kid. Can you believe this kid? He's wild. Three vaginas. God, this guy. I love this guy.

The old man's watching the fire move in waves, throwing everything into shadow. Shadows of shadows.

From the furthest corners to both poles of the earth, I bring to you the circus of circuses! Hezada!

Hezada! yell back the teenagers.

My daughter's dead, says the old man.

What?

My daughter.

What'd he say?

Said his daughter's dead.

No way.

Yeah.

Then what'd Travis say?

Travis takes the old man's elbow. Here, let's sit down, he says.

The old man lets himself be lowered, still watching the fire. Travis looks into the fire, then back at the man. You see her in there? In the bonfire?

The old man looks at him.

Shit. You want another drink? Let me get you a drink. You stay right here. I'll be right back. Get you a drink.

He pats the old man's shoulder, then hurries to the foldout table his mother uses for the annual craft fair. She sells wreaths. He used to go on walks to collect the acorns she glues into them.

Everybody crowds him. What's going on? You know who he is? What about his daughter being dead?

I don't know, I don't know, he says, then hurries back to the fire and sets the full cup in the old man's hand. The old man has thick fingers and big knuckles like his own grandfather. A few of the joints seem to go sideways. Must have worked out in the oil fields too. Or maybe as a mechanic.

Suddenly, the old man stands up. I need to go, he says, nearly falling over and sort of twisting at the waist and catching his hands on the straw bale before trying to stand upright again. A piece of straw splinters under his thumbnail, but he doesn't feel it.

The kid stands up too, keeping his arm around the old man's shoulders. The man drops his cup. It hits the ground and beer splatters.

A girl jumps up, gasping. My new jacket, she says.

I'll get you another, says Travis.

Another jacket? says the girl. And now she's wiping at her legs. The boy with her is mopping her up with the arm of his flannel.

Sure, another jacket, another beer, whatever.

This cost like ninety-five dollars.

Get that geezer out of here, the girl's boyfriend says.

Stay cool, says Travis. His daughter's dead, man. Dead.

Yeah? He don't even know how he got here. What if his daughter's been dead for fifty years? Maybe he don't even have a daughter.

I had a daughter, says the old man.

Sure you did, says Travis, patting his arm.

The boyfriend points at Travis. If you don't get him the fuck out of here, he's gonna be dead too.

Is it your birthday or something? says the old man.

Naw, is it yours? says Travis.

It's not my birthday.

It's the circus party.

Hezada! The kids raise their cups.

Hezada! They drink.

I miss her, the old man says, and covers his face with his hands. He crumples to the ground.

Listen, says Travis. Travis stands back on the bale. Let's have a toast. A toast to our new friend's daughter. C'mon, everybody. Fill your cups. That's right. Fill them up, fill up and come on over here. We're gonna toast a good, dead woman. A good and dead woman. Just kidding. A loving daughter, says Travis, thinking of the white words on granite graves in the cemetery.

The others listen and start gathering around the fire. Travis smiles and clutches his cup of beer against his heart. What was your daughter's name?

Hezada, the old man says.

No, man, your daughter.

The old man looks up at him. You don't know her?

Sure, I do. She was a great gal. I just want to hear you say it, say her name. It'll be good. Good to say it. So we can toast her.

The old man closes his eyes. Kae, he says.

Travis lifts his cup. To Kae!

Did he say Kae?

Oh, fuck. Not that Kae.

What other Kae is there?

There's the lady who runs the thrift store.

That's Kae.

Oh, fuck. That's her…

I didn't know her dad was still alive.

I never thought of her having a dad.

Ask him if it's the same Kae.

The old man is pressing his palms to his eyes.

To Kae! Travis shouts.

The kids lift their cups. To Kae.

Everyone drinks.

The fire crackles.

The old man opens his mouth and vomits.

Oh, shit! someone says.

Gross!

Did he just?

Yeah, he did.

Man, says one kid to another, if I ever, I mean ever, end up like that guy, just shoot me. Promise me.

Sure, I'll shoot you.

The kid holds his fingers to his temple. I mean it. Boom, boom, man. Boom, boom.

A girl pulls her phone from her back pocket and holds it up as she crouches beside the old man.

Here, everybody lean in, she says, gesturing like the school photographer taking a class photo.

What are you doing?

What's it look like I'm doing?

Someone tell her who he is. About Kae. Travis, tell her to stop it. That's the suicide woman's dad.

Travis's eyes widen. Hey, Travis says to the girl. That's not cool.

What, is he your granddaddy all of a sudden?

No he's—

She rolls her eyes.

It's the dead lady's dad.

Whatever it is, she says.

You'll go to hell for this, says Travis.

We already live there, she says and snaps the photo.

But it's too much for some of them, and they wander back to the table. They toss their cups into the black trash bag someone's tied around a tree branch.

Oh man, don't go, says the kid with a smile, when he sees people starting to head toward the parked cars. He spent the whole last week finding someone to buy the kegs, and then all yesterday he was hauling them up here, and this is supposed to be the best party of the summer, and probably the circus people will be here soon. The fire-eater sucking on branches from the bonfire. The jugglers throwing straw bales back and forth. Man, it's their last year of school, last summer before their last year, best summer, best party.

Wait! Wait!

Now the girls are taking turns kissing the old man's cheeks while the girl with a camera moves this way and that way. Bee-oo-tiful, dahling. Be-oot-iful!

Gotta get up early.

I have a good idea, says the boy with a smile. Hear me out, hear me out.

If it's driving to the porn store, don't bother.

We'll go to her house.

Whose house?

Kae's. The woman that offed herself today. The kid smiles. He has no idea what he's thinking until he's saying it, but everybody's stopped. They're listening. So he keeps going. Yeah, go see where she did it. Meet her ghost, maybe.

What are you, five years old, believing in ghosts?

That's some twisted shit.

Hear me out, hear me out.

Man, it just happened. You don't do shit like that, going to a dead woman's house. Have some respect.

Maybe it's not her dad. He had a daughter named Kae—they aren't the same Kae.

Right.

It's just a coincidence.

No such thing as coincidences around here.

Listen, the boy says with a smile, this is like a once-in-a-lifetime thing. It *just* happened, right? Like, don't you want to know?

Know what?

About whether it exists. What happens *after*.

How will going to her house prove anything?

If she's still there, it'll prove a lot, I'd think. Everybody knows suicide is like the worst way to die. If anybody's trapped between worlds, gonna be her.

That makes sense.

Hell if it does.

I'm game.

What if someone killed her?

All the spookier, man.

Count me out.

Oh, come see. What's it hurt?

It's just wrong. And if you can't see that. Well…

It won't hurt a thing. Best time to see a ghost is right after it happens. Night of a death. Night her ghost starts walking. All the ghosts you hear about have been dead for years. But this, man, this is like guar-an-fucking-teed. We would be the very first to see her rising up. Or whatever she does.

Now you're the one who's going to hell.

Thought you said we live there already.

True, true.

They button up their coats. What about the keg? The fire? About the old man?

He asleep?

Yeah.

Leave him here. He'll wake up eventually.

Or we could take him with us.

Your mama did drop you on the head, no question. No question.

Hear me out. She'll recognize her own dad, right? If he's with us, she's more likely to appear.

Not if she hated him.

Did she?

You watch too many ghost shows on TV.

You're crazy, you know? Here, I have an idea. We take him with us but leave you at the circus.

Fuck, he should be in that asylum in Ashmore.

Hezada! shouts the kid with a smile.

Hezada! they shout back.

110

Hezada steps into the silver leotard and pulls it up her legs, over her hips and chest. She slips in one arm, then the other. Usually, Frank helps her fasten the peacock feathers onto the back. Maybe she'll wait until he's good and surprised at the swimming pool, and then ask if he'll do it. Of course, when she had good use of her arms she fastened them herself. And before her, she fastened her mother's when she was old enough to manipulate the closures.

She drapes the blue velvet cloak over her shoulders. She used to wear it into the ring, the whole tent dark except one spotlight following her. Like God held a flashlight only on her. That's how she felt sometimes.

The whole tent would go quiet as the darkness.

She would stop.

So quiet that everybody could recognize whose baby let out a cry.

Then the cloak would fall to her feet.

There was a costumer in New York who made the Hezada costumes. She remembers riding the train with her mother out there to be fitted in a new wardrobe. Was her grandmother there too? She tries to remember who sat by whom. Her grandmother's costumes are in one of the regional circus museums.

She begins walking up the midway.

It's late, but the circus feels empty.

She should have told Frank about the party. But the circus boss was so delighted and begged her not to say.

She wanted to say, There's joy without surprise too. But how could he understand that?

She thought of the little girl Frank brought by this afternoon.

We're going to ride the Ferris wheel, he said. You want to come?

And she and Frank looked at each other, and she knew he feared this girl would try to run away with them.

I'd love to, she said. What's your name?

Heza.

That feels like an unlikely coincidence.

Heza stared up at her.

My name's Hezada.

The girl nodded.

Neither knew the other.

111

The line of cars and trucks is driving fast from the circus party, veering onto the country road that heads into the village.

A red reflector flashes by. Then another.

When she was a kid, she'd press her forehead against the back window of her parents' car, counting reflectors on the ride home from Wednesday night church. She likes how the ones out here appear and disappear without the rhythm that reflectors have on highways. Just focus on those. And breathe. Don't get sick. She closes her eyes. Her head reels. She opens her eyes. And don't close your eyes.

Something touches her side. Somebody. She shifts away, folding her arms closer against her waist. The fingers continue, moving up her ribs. She swats at them. They pause. Then begin climbing again.

Dashboard lights.

Laughter.

A red reflector flashes. Gone.

It was a small church her parents went to. Still go to. She hasn't gone in a while, or hadn't until last week. The idea of going was better than the actual going. But her mother seemed proud. She talks about you all the time, a churchgoer confided, clenching her hand. The woman's fingers were bony, her whole life behind her eyes.

Now the hand's at the side of her breast. She punches at it. Quit it! she hisses.

The sound of the road goes on and on beneath her, under the floorboard, trembling under her feet.

Now the hand's kneading her breast. If she could reach, she'd bite it off. Rip it right off the arm. Everybody's having a good time.

Whose hand is this? Who are these people even?

God, she feels sick. Wouldn't be the first time she's thrown up on the side of a country road. Wonder if there's an internet article about that.

She thinks of standing beside her grandmother at the kitchen table, her grandmother's hands circling the flour. Her grandmother flips the dough. I want to be like you, she says, but her grandmother can't hear through memory.

Her grandmother has strong arms, sure hands. She wears a thin housedress that snaps down the front.

Like this, her grandmother says.

Like this? she says.

Her grandmother pauses to watch her try.

Almost, her grandmother says. Watch again.

More hands are on her. She squeezes her arms against her sides, trapping the fingers for a moment. She tries to become a vice and break them.

Somebody hits her in the face.

Are we there yet? she says.

Are we there yet? she says, louder.

Please, she says.

Are we there, are we there, are we there.

112

When's Frank gonna be here?

Who's bringing him?

Maybe he's at his mom's.

Where's she live?

He always visits her the first day of the last circus.

Does this day count?

Yeah, the first day being the arriving day. That's what I mean.

Circus boss said Frank wasn't going to go until after the circus was over. When he was done.

That's unlike him.

It won't be the circus without Frank, I'll tell you what.

Maybe that's good, yeah? Maybe that's exactly what the circus needs. To shut down for good and ever.

113

When the teenagers and their headlights reach the edge of the circus field, they begin slowing down, weeds and cornstalks losing their blur, until they're moving slow as a funeral procession.

Under the circus entrance sit the ticket booths. Their windows are shuttered, but the lights flash. The tops of tents rise darkly behind the sign.

You think the elephants can hear us?

Only one elephant anymore.

You think it hears us, though?

Probably. Ears like that, sure.

How far you think it can hear? Like across-the-ocean far? Or just from-here-to-Charleston far? Here-to-Chicago far?

Maybe it can hear into the past.

No way. Do you really think that?

Maybe.

The caravan of kids rolls on past the circus and down one neighborhood street and up another.

Anybody know where she lives?

Lived.

You know what I mean.

Turn up there, says one of the girls, squeezing between two front seats. I used to babysit her kids.

Kids?

Yeah, a boy and a girl. Twins. They're nice kids. Pretty funny, actually.

Wait. It's *their* mom?

Kae.

I didn't know her name.

Travis didn't say anything about kids.

He might not have known, or cared. You know him.

It'll be fine. It's not like the kids will be there.

How do you know?

Nobody's leaving two little kids at home alone the same day their mom did that.

I hear suicide's catching. That's why news channels don't broadcast it. So it's happening a ton, but, like, nobody knows because the media won't talk about it.

You're making it up.

I'm not. It's not true that it's catching like the flu or something, but for a long time people thought so.

How do you know so much about it, anyway?

Health class. Where were you?

That's the house, says the former babysitter. The yellow one.

I don't like this.

Get out if you don't like it, then.

Maybe I will.

The cars pull up to the curb. The yard's full of puddles. The windows are dark. They cut their engines. This is the house.

Anybody know where it happened?

Ask her ghost, you moron, says one of the kids and pushes open the door and walks off. They watch him in the side mirrors until he's so far up the street they know he's not coming back.

Whatever.

I agree, let's just drop this guy and go.

The kids lean over the old man, trying to maneuver him out of the car. He starts to slide out. They catch him before his knees hit the curb.

He groans but doesn't wake up.

Amazing.

Hezada, someone says.

They crouch on either side of him, hooking his arms around their necks, holding his wrists to keep him from slipping.

They drag him to the porch and set him up in the chair there.

He looks like a goddamned scarecrow, but he's heavy as fuck.

Where'd you learn to talk like that?

My mommy.

They laugh.

It has been a good night, after all.

I have to pee, says the babysitter.

Hold it.

I can't hold it.

Are you fucking kidding me?

I won't take long. Just wait.

Before anybody can lock the car doors, she's out and hurrying around the house to the back door because it's never locked.

114

You hear that? Abe says.

Heza listens.

That, he says.

Heza looks in the direction he's looking. Sounds like someone's on the back steps.

Heza starts walking to the back door. Faster. But slowing down in the kitchen so her boots don't slip. She flips on the porchlight.

Their mother stands there, smiling, laughing. She taps at the door window, pointing down at the lock.

C'mon, Heza, she says. Unlock the door.

Heza's three or four and has just learned that she's tall enough to reach the lock and flip it shut, and that if she does it while her mom's outside, her mom will make super funny faces and sounds. And then, when she unlocks the door, she runs away before her mom can sweep her up into a torrent of tickles.

Once, her mother ran around the house and came through the front door, then crept to the kitchen, sneaking up behind Heza.

Boo!

Heza screamed, then seeing it was her mother, began to cry. Her mother picked her up, rocking her. You're safe, baby. You're safe.

Heza goes back into the living room where Abe sits on the couch.

Was somebody there?

No, she says. Nobody was there. Let's go to bed.

115

Frank dreams that he's driving the camper up the road, and in the rear-view mirror, the road goes on and on.

116

The babysitter tests the back door. The knob turns with her hand.

Good.

She crouches down and slides off her sneakers. Some of the old man's vomit is on the left one. She carefully steps inside, leaving the door slightly ajar in case the kids are here and asleep. She just needs to pee. If she weren't on her period, she would've peed in the back alley.

Even if the kids are here, and they do wake up and find her, hopefully they won't be scared since they know her. She watched them more frequently when their mom was dating, but surely they'll remember her. If they wake up, she'll lead them back to their bedrooms and read them a story until they fall asleep. Maybe she'll fall asleep too. Sleep sounds good.

She makes her way around the kitchen to the stairs. Even if she'd never been in the house, she'd know her way since so many village houses have the same layout.

Why didn't she just knock and ask Heza if she could use their bathroom? Heza probably would have said yes.

Because we've abducted their grandfather, that's why.

Because Travis is looking up séances online so he can lead one in the garage.

Because she's a badass for daring to come in here.

Because there feels to be a vastness around Heza and Abe, a kind of oceanic silence that causes everyone to move quietly around them, to stay back, to think of a thousand words to say but say none.

She can feel blood rush into her underwear as she climbs the stairs. She lets her fingertips brush the banister.

At the top of the stairs, she pauses and listens for the children.

117

Heza and Abe lie under the comforter on their mother's bed. It's thick and white, covered in red roses like the tattooed lady. Heza traces one. She thinks of Jude. On the back of their mother's bedroom door is her bathrobe.

Abe picks up one of their mother's hairs. He holds it between the fingers of both hands.

Did she leave a note? Abe says.

Heza doesn't answer.

Heza? Abe says.

She closes her eyes.

I know you hear me, he says.

I hear you.

Did she?

Yeah.

Let me see it.

I don't have it.

Who has it? Grandma?

Police, I guess.

What they want it for?

Heza shrugs.

Like forever?

I don't know.

Did you read it?

Yeah.

Abe waits.

Heza looks at her hands.

The streetlights through the lace curtains make patterns on the carpet.

Tell me, Heza. What'd it say?

She tells him.

It was her handwriting?

Yes, but fragile.

They fall asleep quickly after that.

118

The bathroom light switch is not where the babysitter remembers. But the little windows let in enough moonlight to see by. She lets her eyes adjust, then she sits on the toilet. Only a thin square of toilet paper remains on the cardboard roll. She leans forward to open the sink cabinet, but there's only toilet bowl cleaner and a box of tampons with SUPER written on a green banner flying across the box. She takes one.

She uses the tiny bit of toilet paper and shakes her hips to dry best she can before standing and pulling up her underwear. Bits of straw and grass fall from her hair and jacket onto the furry blue mat. She bends down and tries picking up the mess and sprinkling them into the toilet.

Should she flush?

She wasn't going to, but now there's field in the water. And blood.

She could climb into the shower, reach out and flush the toilet, then pull her hand back behind the curtain and wait. If the kids run into the bathroom, she'll hold her breath until they leave.

But if she doesn't flush the toilet, tomorrow morning they'll wonder why there's bits of blood and field in the toilet. Might even notice the tampon wrapper. They'll think it has something to do with their mother. And that seems wrong. Leaving clues that aren't clues.

Maybe they won't think about it.

Probably they will.

She reaches up and pushes the curtain's metal rings against the rod to keep them from whining as she steps in. She climbs into the tub. There's rubbery starfish stuck on the bottom. She flushes the toilet, pulls her arm inside the curtain, and waits.

119

Cold night, someone says.

Warmer in the water, someone else says.

Ada lies in one of the swimming pool lounge chairs. She curls her knees closer to her chest. The chill moves into her dreams, or whatever layer of consciousness she's wading through. She is and isn't here, though she can feel the hard plastic beneath her. She's not worried about Jude since Davey texted her a picture of Jude sleeping, hands under her cheek.

Ada sent a heart back.

You okay? came the next text.

Yeah, she typed back.

I'm sorry, came the next.

Now her phone's in her apron, and her apron is with her shoes under the chair.

Hezada the Great is jumping off the high dive in her silver costume sewn with a million little moons. Or Hezada the Great is naked, and someone else is wearing her costume and diving. Is that Jude up there? Maybe it's Kae. That'd be like Kae's ghost to dress up in a sequined leotard.

Hezada surfaces in the water. Then climbs out of the pool. She's beautiful.

Beautiful, Ada whispers.

Hezada begins walking around the concrete toward the lounge chairs. She sits down on the one next to Ada, then brings her feet up and leans back. Some of the pool water flicks onto Ada.

Sorry about that.

It's okay. I've always been a big fan.

Thanks.

Since I was a little kid.

Sure.

Hezada's legs are strong and lean. Not how Ada imagined them. Older women are always more beautiful in person than she ever imagines they are. Why is that?

Ada looks for a gap in Hezada's costume, a ripple that might serve as peephole to see whether a breast lies there like a dove.

If it's there, she's back in time, before she was born and Hezada was young. What was that like? Probably not as beautiful as the stories. Surely, everyone would have leered at Hezada then too, her confidence over gravity, her daring costumes, her smile wide with a belief in herself that the audience innately doubted, imagining her breaking against the ground no matter how many times she didn't.

Would it be impolite to ask?

The children did not investigate the sound of the toilet flushing. And when the babysitter is sure that they won't, and even more sure, she sneaks down the stairs and out of the house, nearly fainting when she sees the old man slumped on the front porch where they left him sleeping, chin on his chest. A pile of mourning gifts near him—plants, cookies piled under plastic wrap, a package of toilet paper, paper towels, flowers dyed neon pink, grocery bags lined up like luminaries holding candy bags, baggies, whatever the villagers could think of as they pushed their carts through the grocery, gathering offerings.

The babysitter hurries up the street to where the car's parked. She climbs in.

I thought you'd leave me, she said.

We thought you'd died or something.

I'm fine. Let's go, let's go.

What's it like in there?

It's a house like anybody's.

Shut up.

It's not like I took a tour or anything. I had to pee.

What was it like?

She shrugs. She thinks of the toothpaste on the bathroom sink, the orange bottles of pills in a basket with the Kae's name on them. The tube of lipstick that she took from the bathroom sink cabinet, even though she doesn't wear lipstick. She touches it inside her jacket pocket, and rolls it against her fingers.

121

The twins don't hear the car drive off, or the other trucks and cars driving by. They sleep through the sounds of someone trying to open the garage door before giving up and returning to the dark and more trucks and cars that veer down the alley and up the streets.

But the tiger hears, despite its cage.

123

It's real beautiful, the circus field under the moonlight. Real beautiful, and easy to imagine the tents and trees floating out in the middle of some warm midnight ocean. Easy to imagine it's what everyone sleeping in the village is dreaming, all of them dreaming this dream before morning comes and they wander through the tents, searching for it.

The night's graying toward dawn when Frank wakes up in the old man's car. The old man's not there. The pine tree deodorizer hangs from the rear-view mirror. Frank's got a crick in his neck and down one side. Used to take a day, maybe two of sleeping right before he'd feel better. Anymore, he might have to find a chiropractor. He has one in Florida, but not up here. Same with the dentist. His doctor. The men who fish on the dock every morning.

He gets out of the car. It's the only one in the lot. So quiet. So empty. He listens for birds.

Might be sunrise before he gets back to his camper, but that's okay. It's been a long time since he saw that. Really saw that.

There's the band shell, the playground, the horseshoes.

There's the swimming pool.

There's the early dawn shapes of people inside the swimming pool. Probably teenagers sneaking in to skinny-dip. He follows the chain-link fence to the entrance.

The pool's metal gates are pushed open, so just anybody could wander in. Above the counter hangs a banner that reads FRANK! in large letters. On the counter is a jar of gold kazoos. He picks one up. Happy 50th! is printed on it. He slips it in his pocket, then walks through the changing room that leads out to the pool area.

NO RUNNING is stenciled in yellow paint on the concrete.

A five-layer cardboard cake sits on wheels by the lifeguard station.

In the kiddie pool sit two clowns in full costume. One's asleep. The other's awake, but blinking slowly.

An acrobat is crouched and picking up bits of broken glass.

A kid with a smile on his face is floating in a life-saver ring.

Someone's on the high dive, dead or asleep.

A woman comes out of the dressing room, then goes back in.

Over by the closed concession stand sit the jugglers at the stone picnic table. It's littered with beer bottles and fast-food wrappers.

Frank! Frank!

It's about time you got here, you old son-of-a.

Hey, it is Frank. Happy retirement, you.

The jugglers move their soft drinks to clear a space for him. They smell like bar, cigarettes, and hamburger grease. Add a whiff of cotton candy, face paint, and animal, and it'd be the circus.

We was thinking you'd never get here. Thought maybe you'd run away from the circus.

Hey, somebody get this man a burger.

The man of the hour! The man of the circus! The man of a life-time! The man after my own heart. Get him a burger.

You want cheese, Frank? You'd think they'd be marked for convenience. You a cheese man, Frank?

We're out of burgers.

Check again.

A juggler picks up the paper bag, blows into it, then smashes it with a mighty bang. The acrobat looks up.

Like a goddamned man in a cannon. I bet Frank remembers those days. Do you, Frank?

What a liability.

People didn't sue back then.

Frankie, were you ever shot out of a cannon?

Once or twice, Frank says.

God, those were the good old days, weren't they?

Boss around? Frank says.

One of the guys points at a lifeguard chair.

There he is, up in the lifeguard chair, tuxedo tail trailing down the ladder. His camera hangs off his neck, lens against his bare belly.

Pretty soon, the sky will be just right for pictures. Then not again until about twilight.

Where you going, Frank?

Did you get a kazoo? Picture of your face on every kazoo. When you got here, he was gonna hand them out like cigars.

Where you going, Frankie?

Reckon there's a few hours of sleep left in my camper.

Here's an idea. We've got the banner. And the kazoos. We'll pretend you were never here. And we'll try it all again tomorrow.

Frank heads back toward the entrance. He learned to swim in a pool like this. By this afternoon, the green plastic lounge chairs will be draped in sun-lotioned mothers, sky drifting across their sunglasses as their kids do cannonballs and belly-flops off the diving boards.

In the last two chairs lie two women. One has her arms crossed and the elastic on her bikini bottoms is shot at the waist. A waitress, the way her mouth tugs downward.

Against the fence leans the fan of peacock feathers.

Hezada lies in the other green chair. She's stretched out under her blue cloak, hands crossed over her chest like usual when she sleeps. He's never liked seeing her sleep like that. Her hair's damp. He imagines her treading in the midnight water, her costume's sequins lifting like a mermaid's scales.

He leans in and whispers in her ear.

She opens her eyes.

ACKNOWLEDGMENTS

Thank you to my sister for taking me to the circus.

Thank you to Jeremy, who found the phrase *Hezada, I Miss You* on a bathroom wall, wrote it on a scrap of paper, and brought it home to me. Here it is, Jeremy.

All my love to Heather, who helped create time for me to write this. I'm sorry this book was so hard. It's done now. For now.

Thank you to Pam Larratt for being my first reader, week by week, until the chapters were finally out and threaded.

Thank you to Jack and Jeremy for reading the book when it wouldn't leave me alone.

Special thanks to Amy Sinclair for letting me consult her on our regionalisms.

Shout out to the baristas who made my daily writing space warm and welcoming: Stephanie, Jocelyn, Naomi, and Brooke.

And, not least, my deep gratitude to Tatiana Ryckman for saying yes to the book, and to all the fine people at Awst who have treated the story with great interest and care: LK, Emily, Phoebe, and Wendy.

ABOUT THE AUTHOR

Erin Pringle grew up in Casey, Illinois. She is the author of two story collections, *The Floating Order* (Two Ravens Press, 2009) and *The Whole World at Once* (Vandalia Press/West Virginia University Press, 2017), as well as several chapbooks and a hundred or more stories. Along the way, she has received financial support from the Rose fellowship at Texas State University, and an Artist Trust fellowship from the Washington State arts organization of the same name. In addition to writing, Erin loves to run, swim, and read. She teaches children's tennis and preschool art, and co-hosts an interview program on KYRS Thin Air Community Radio. She lives in Spokane, Washington with her partner, Heather, and son, Henry Valentine.

Learn more about Erin and her work at erinpringle.com

READING AND DISCUSSION QUESTIONS

1. What memories do you have of the circus, and how did those affect your reading of *Hezada, I Miss You*?

2. Much of the United States' cultural landscape, if not also its nostalgic landscape, was affected by the travelling circus—from its forms of entertainment and methods of advertising to its modes of imagination. The circus continues to grip the modern imagination. Why do you think that is?

3. Like the circus, suicide is often romanticized in art. Why do you think that is? How is suicide presented in *Hezada! I Miss You*?

4. Most novels and fictions contain both heroes and villains/protagonists and antagonists. It's more difficult to find clear heroes and villains in *Hezada! I Miss You*. Why do you think that is?

5. What scene stood out most to you, and why?

6. Which character did you find most compelling, and why?

7. What kinds of stories do you think people need in the 21st century? How does *Hezada!* fit into the discussion?

8. How would you describe the relationship between the circus and the village?

9. In the novel, it becomes increasingly difficult to identify why Kae died in the way she did. However, many of the characters seem drawn to finding a clear explanation. Why do you think this is?

10. In what ways do you see the circus and the village shaping the way the characters view themselves and others?

11. At the end of the novel, Hezada is posed in sleep as one about to be buried. What did you make of this?

12. How would you describe the relationship between Hezada and Kae, between their lives in the circus/village, between their pasts and presents?

13. Consider how the women's bodies are treated in the novel. What patterns do you notice?

14. One of the invisible but driving forces in the novel is the economic decay of the circus and village and their wish to find stability through tourism and audiences. Where else do you see economics shaping the ways the characters behave toward, and view, themselves and/or their world? What other invisible forces seem to shape the characters' lives?

15. What do you think the children's behaviors show us about the environment of people and ideas they're growing up in?

16. What other works does *Hezada!* remind you of?

17. Imagine you're on a bus reading this novel. A stranger asks what it's about. How would you explain it?

18. Like attending the circus, reading novels is often considered an escape from reality. Do you think that's accurate? How would you describe the experience of reading *Hezada! I Miss You*?

19. The people of the village and the circus seem to occupy a place that is suspended somewhere between past and present, nostalgia and modernity. In what ways do these themes inform your reading of the work?